HUNGRY GUNS

Buck Larew rode into trouble when he hit the cow country where his brother John was ranching. It was Kansas, wild, dangerous and raw. But Buck had lately turned in his Ranger badge down in Texas, and there was no tougher set-up anywhere than along the Rio Grande. But he didn't want to get drawn into trouble. He'd ridden north to get away from that. Yet his brother was in danger, and there wasn't a man anywhere better fitted to handle it than Buck Larew. So he took a hand and came up against the scheming Ben Lazzard and the tough outfit that lived under the brand of the Lazy L. The hungry guns were satisfied by the time the shooting stopped.

HUNGRY GUNS

by

BURT KROLL

ROBERT HALE · LONDON

© Burt Kroll 1967

First published in Great Britain 1967

Reprinted 1983

ISBN 0 7090 1056 7

Robert Hale Limited
Clerkenwell House
Clerkenwell Green
London EC1R 0HT

Printed in Great Britain by
Photobooks (Bristol) Limited
Barton Manor, St. Philips, Bristol
and bound by
W.B.C. Bookbinders Limited

CHAPTER 1

IT SURE was a big country, Buck Larew thought, reining
up on a crest and easing himself in his saddle. He stared
around through narrowed brown eyes, his hatbrim pulled
low against the glare of the sun. He'd ridden all morning
and most of the afternoon across this range from Rainbow Creek, and he still hadn't spotted sign of the Bar 60
ranch, owned by his brother John. He didn't think he'd
lost his way. He had a good sense of direction, having
been a Texas Ranger for five years before deciding to
throw in his hand with the law and come up to Kansas
to help his brother run the ranch. He hadn't seen John
in several years, and had been most reluctant to make
the big change from law dealing to ranching, but having
taken the plunge, he was now anxious to get settled into
his new life.

A gunshot echoed thinly in the distance and he
stiffened and peered around. His dark eyes narrowed still
more when he caught a glimpse of movement far away in
the middle distance. The glare from the sun didn't help
him, but he spotted dust rising, and saw that it was moving fast to the left. More shots rang out, sounding puny
and insignificant from this distance, and Larew spurred
his horse and went forward quickly. Someone was in
trouble, and his training as a lawman and his instincts as
a man made him want to find out what was happening.

He galloped down a long slope, and thinned his lips
when he saw a fence stretching across the range from
right to left. The fence was broken. He could see half a
dozen posts down, and the wire was trampled into the

grass. Dust was wisping on the bright air, and in the distance and still moving away fast were half a dozen riders. He halted at the fence and placed both his hands on his saddlehorn, leaning the weight of his upper body upon them. There was a cold thought in his mind. He had come upon troubled range.

Hoofbeats sounded close by and he twisted in his saddle to see a couple of riders coming up from the right. He remained motionless and the two newcomers galloped right up to him, with guns in their hands. They hauled their mounts to a slithering halt on the other side of the fallen fence, and Larew took in their angry faces.

The man on the right was past middle-age, a wide shouldered man whose heavy frame still possessed great strength. His craggy face was harshly set, his dark eyes glinting, and there was no mistaking the anger that was coursing through him.

"Throw 'em up," he called. "Don't make a move."

The other man was taller, and thin, almost a bean-pole in his saddle. But he looked dangerous, and the gun in his hand was steady as a rock. His pale eyes bored into Larew.

"I said get 'em up," the heavier man snapped. "At last I've got one of you."

"I figure you're making a mistake," Larew drawled. He glanced to the left. The riders were gone now, but dust still marked their trail. "The way I see it a bunch of riders just tore down this fence. They headed off that way. You figure that I'm one of them."

"That's right," the older man said, easing his heavy bulk in the saddle. His horse moved a couple of steps to counter-act the shifting weight. "I suppose you're gonna tell me that you don't know a damn thing about it."

"That's right," Larew said. "You don't figure I'd sit my hoss here while all the others got away, do you?"

"Who are you?" the thin man cut in.

"That's better." Larew smiled tightly. "I'm Buck Larew. I'm looking for the Bar Sixty, owned by my brother John."

"Larew!" The big man sent his horse across the trailing strands of wire, lowering his gun as he did so. But his harsh face did not relax. "Are you the ex-Texas Ranger who might help us out of this trouble?"

"I don't know what my brother has promised around here on my behalf," Buck said in clipped tones. "But if he's in any kind of trouble I'll surely help him out."

"I'm Wire Sutton, of the Broken S," the big man said heavily. "This is Rake Foster, my foreman. We're having plenty of trouble from the Lazzards. They own the Lazy L over that way. Ben and his son Ike. A couple of no-good bums. If they didn't run such a tough crew we'd take them and hang 'em."

"Easier said than done," Rake Foster put in. He holstered his gun and came across the broken wire. "Glad to know you, Larew. If you're half the man your brother says then our troubles are halfway over."

"Just hold up a bit," Buck said. "I ain't making any promises. If you know who is making this trouble for you why haven't you got the law on to him? You've got some law in this county, haven't you?"

"Bub Wickup wears the sheriff's badge," Sutton said, stepping to the ground and trailing his reins. He came to the head of Larew's horse and stared up at Buck. His harsh face was fleshy, his puffy eyelids almost hooding the dark eyes out of sight. "When you see Wickup you'll know we ain't got no law around here."

"Lee Paine ain't so bad," Foster supplied. "He's the deputy. But he don't get no support from the sheriff nor the town."

"I came through Rainbow Creek," Larew said. "I

didn't see the law. How far am I from my brother's place?"

"We'll ride with you," Sutton said. "The house is about five miles to the north. I want to have a talk with John. Now that you're here we better start making plans. Your brother is expecting you, and he told us to hold up until you got here."

"So you want to push me into some kind of a range war?" Larew shook his head. "I figured that I was coming here to do some cow nursing. Didn't know John was having some trouble."

"He'll tell you all about it when you see him," Sutton said curtly. "But I'll tell you this much. You're lucky you've got a brother here waiting for you. He was dry-gulched a couple of weeks ago, and took a bullet through his right shoulder. A couple of inches more to the left and it would have got him dead centre. Someone was trying to kill him, and that might not be the end of it."

"You mentioned the Lazzards," Larew said, his face now grim. "Are you sure they're behind the shooting?"

"Sure as hell, but we can't prove it." Sutton climbed back into his saddle. "Come on, we'll ride with you to your brother's place. No sense us trying to get them jaspers who pulled down this fence. We'd never catch up with them. Even if we did there's nothing we can do about them. They're too strong for us."

Larew was thoughtful as he accompanied the two men across the range. John hadn't mentioned trouble at all in any of his frequent letters. But perhaps that was why his brother had been eager to get him here in Kansas. Buck Larew was a fast man with a gun. But he couldn't believe that his brother would want him to come up here and get into trouble. By the sounds of it a tough bunch was kicking up the dust, and the fact that the law was weak made it all the worse. But something would have to be done about the trouble-makers. If they were left to their tricks someone would get killed before it was done.

"It ain't a pleasant home-coming for you," Wire Sutton said.

"That's damn true," Larew retorted. "But why haven't the rest of you ranchers got together against this tough bunch? That's the way trouble on the range is usually handled. Ain't there enough of you to gang up on the Lazzards?"

"You've hit the nail on the head," Rake Foster said. "The rest of the ranchers don't agree. Some of them ain't being touched, and they ain't likely to buy into something that don't affect them. They can't see any farther than the ends of their noses. They don't know that this kind of trouble can spread, and fast. By the time they do get dragged into it they'll be too slow to do anything about it."

"What started it?" Larew demanded.

"That damn, hell-raising son of Ben Lazzard," Sutton cursed. "Your brother was planning to marry Letty Haig, whose father owns the H7 on the other side of the Bar Sixty. Then Ike Lazzard got the notion that he'd like to marry Hetty, and he started acting up around your brother. But John Larew fought him into the dust, and put a bullet through Ike's gunhand into the bargain. That didn't go down well with Ben Lazzard, and the Lazy L started riding your brother, looking for an excuse to smoke him into hell. He wouldn't bite on that though, and the whole county knows that he ain't gonna get his head blowed off by that salty bunch. He's playing it right, although it takes a real man to take that kind of a situation. They wait around town for him, and hoorah him, but he won't bite. I figure mebbe he's been waiting for you to show up, Larew. Now the two of you will get together mebbe we'll see some action around here. I'll tell you this much. Me and my boys are ready to back you up. Have a talk with John, and if you decide to go out for the Lazzards then we'll come along. I've had some trouble. I held off that Lazy L bunch when they had your brother on the ground. If I hadn't made my play John would be dead now."

"I'm thanking you for that," Buck Larew said. "I'll sure help out all I can. But I'll have a word with John before making any promises."

"Shouldn't want you to handle it any other way," Sutton said. "But I just wanted you to know how it stands."

"It looks stacked pretty high to me," Larew said. "But there must be some way this can be roped down. I don't think anyone would score if it came to out and out shooting."

"You'll get the hang of it," Sutton said, "being a lawman, you'll know how it shapes up."

They continued, and the dusty miles dropped by. Larew could see that they were crossing fine rangeland, and he kept staring around, watching for signs of trouble. If there were hungry guns around here then they wouldn't take long to get into action. He didn't like the idea of drawing into a fight, but if his brother was in trouble then he would have no option but to fight.

They breasted a rise and reined in, and Larew saw a collection of buildings far below, standing on a small shelf about half way down the long slope.

"That's the Bar Sixty," Sutton said. "Look, we shan't come in with you right now. You ain't seen your brother in years, and you don't want me hanging around waiting to talk turkey. Tell John I'll be riding over some time tomorrow to talk, and then we'll get down to business. How's that?"

"It'll do fine," Larew said, "and thanks for your help."

"I'm hoping that I'll have to say that to you before very long," the big rancher said, wheeling his horse away. "Better tell your brother that if we don't get started soon on fighting this set-up it'll be too damn late to do anything. The whole business is shaping up to a bad war."

"See you later," Larew said, and gigged his mount forward. He went down the slope and cut across to the house that was sheltered by a stand of trees. He saw a man standing in the doorway of the little barn, and when the man spotted him he disappeared for a moment, to show himself again holding a Winchester. Larew was under the menace of the long gun as he rode up.

"Howdy," the man greeted. "Who the hell are you?"

"Buck Larew. Is my brother around?"

"He sure is." The cowboy's distant manner broke quickly, and a wide grin came to the lean face as the rifle muzzle was lowered. "John has been waiting weeks for sight of you."

"How is he?" Larew demanded. "I heard that he'd been bushwhacked."

"He's on the mend. I'm Johnny Thorne. I'm the only rider your brother's got."

"Glad to know you, Johnny," Larew responded.

"Saw two riders with you up top there, and they pulled back," the cowboy said. "I thought for a moment that we had some trouble coming. I'd say it was long overdue."

"Bad as that, huh?" Larew demanded, dismounting and trailing his reins. He told the cowboy about the incident at Sutton's fence.

"Yeah," Thorne said in rasping tones. "That's the way it's going around here now. Sure will come to fighting before it's over."

Larew started across the yard for the house. He was impatient to see his brother now, and already there was great pleasure leaping inside him. He and John had always been close, but John had come north to Kansas to start ranching while Buck had stayed behind in Texas to fight for the law. Now it looked as if they would be back together again, and Larew was hoping that the local situation wouldn't do anything to harm the apparently rosy future.

A tall figure appeared in the doorway of the house as he neared it, and he didn't need a second glance to recognise his brother John. He was five years younger than John, and his brother was heavier, older looking. His right arm was in a sling, and he was holding his shoulder stiffly. John Larew was thirty-five years old, and his dark eyes were filled with worry as he emerged into the sunlight. For a moment he stared at Buck, then expression showed on his face and he came forward quickly.

"Buck, it is you!"

"Sure is, old hoss!" Buck replied, mounting the three porch steps and grasping his brother's left hand. "How's it going? You ain't too badly hurt, are you?"

"It ain't worrying me now," John Larew responded. "Come on into the house out of this pesky sun and tell me how you've been making out. I was beginning to think that you'd never show up here. You've been promising and promising."

Buck followed his brother into the house, and sighed his relief when the shade felt cooler. But some of his pleasure had evaporated. John was looking pale and ill, and there was worry on his usually carefree face. This trouble must be worse than even Sutton had made it appear. John usually took everything in his stride.

"Sit down, Buck, and I'll get you a drink," his brother said, and went out back while Buck sat down at the kitchen table. When he came back he was carrying a bucket, and from it he took a couple of bottles. He fetched a couple of glasses, and filled them with cold beer. Buck grinned as he took a glass, but there was no mirth in him. He emptied the glass with a couple of long gulps, and smacked his lips as he set the glass back on the table.

"I hear you're having a lot of trouble around here, John," he said slowly, and gave his brother an account of what had happened and what had been said. His brother nodded from time to time, and his face seemed to get harsher. When Buck lapsed into silence, John said :

"Sutton ain't given you the rights of it, Buck. It's worse than even he knows, and that sounded bad enough just now, coming from you. I wish you hadn't decided to come here. You might only get yourself killed. The best thing you can do is get on your hoss and ride out again, before anything else happens."

"Now wait a minute," Buck said easily. "I came here to do some ranching. If you've got trouble then it's my trouble as well, and I'll soon take a hand if you've got some saddle-bullies in this country. There's only one way to handle them."

"You wouldn't scare the Lazzards into playing it quiet," John Larew said tightly. "I tried that, and I can tell you that they don't scare easy." He glanced down at his bandaged shoulder. "They sure tried to scare me, too, but that didn't work. But I'm about ready to give up and give 'em best."

"What kind of talk is that, and from you?" Buck demanded. "Hell, John, I never thought I'd see the day you'd back down."

"It just ain't worth getting killed for," John Larew said. "I can sell out here and settle some place else."

"You've been here about five years," Buck protested. "It's taken you a time to settle in and start building up. You'd put yourself back a long time if you pulled your stakes now. Don't you worry about a thing. If you've got trouble around here I'll help you shoot it."

"And likely get yourself killed," John retorted. "No, Buck. I already made up my mind to quit."

"What made you decide?" Buck demanded. "How have they got at you, John?"

"I was gonna get married next month," John Larew said thinly. "But Letty has called it off. She doesn't want to see me killed by the Lazzards, and that was what would have happened if she went through with it."

"You mean to tell me you let that bunch dictate terms to you?" Buck demanded. He leaned forward and stared at his brother. "I can't believe it, John," he said. "Look, why don't you start at the beginning and tell me all about it? Let me figure out what's going on, and then we'll do something about it."

"You've got a right to say what should happen," his brother told him, "seeing that you own half the spread. But I don't think I want to stay on here now. The joy has gone out of it. This slug I took from the ambush has done something to me."

"I can understand that," Buck said tightly. "I've been hit more than once, and the first time it happened to me I thought my nerve had gone for good, but it came back. Give yourself time to get over it, John."

"Let's leave it to talk over later," John Larew said, getting to his feet. "You must be tired after your trip. I'll show you to your room, and you can get cleaned up. But keep a gun close to hand. We've been getting some trouble from riders. The other night a couple of gunmen rode by and tossed some slugs into the place."

"We'll soon discourage that," Buck said spiritedly. "You just quit your worrying. Now I'm here you're gonna see a difference."

"Just so long as they don't kill you," John Larew said steadily. "Come on."

Buck followed his brother up the stairs, and glanced around the room into which he was shown. He grinned tiredly, and dropped down on to the bed.

"I could sure do with a long sleep," he said. "It was a hard ride up here."

"You couldn't get here fast enough for me," his brother responded. "I've sure been looking forward to seeing you."

Buck grinned. He got up and moved to the window, staring out across the range. The glare of the sun was lessening. He narrowed his eyes as he spotted movement far out, but he couldn't make out details. He threw a glance at his brother, who was looking over his shoulder.

"You expecting company?" he demanded. "You've sure got some coming in."

"I spotted them," John said tightly. "I ain't expecting anyone."

"Let's get set just in case they ain't friendly," Buck said. He eased his Colt and checked the dusty weapon. Then he started from the room, and his brother followed.

"No shooting, Buck," John Larew said firmly. "It'll only bring on the troubles that much worse. I've been holding off for a long time now."

"But you didn't at the outset," Buck said easily. "Okay, brother, you stick inside the house and quit worrying. If anyone is coming in here to cause trouble then I'll have something to say and do about it."

He passed through the house and reached the porch. He saw Johnny Thorne standing by the barn, the Winchester in the cowboy's hands, and he motioned for the man to get back out of sight. The sound of hoofs was loud now, and a moment later a trio of riders appeared at the gate. They came into the yard, slowing their mounts and looking around.

John Larew was standing in the doorway. Buck tossed a glance at his brother.

"Well, John?" he demanded. "Who are they?"

"Ben Lazzard and a couple of his gunmen," John Larew said tightly. "Don't force any trouble with them, Buck. They are tough men."

"You're scaring me," Buck replied, and leaned against a porch post. His right hand hung down at his side, and the inside of his wrist was against the black butt of his Colt. He narrowed his eyes as the three men came across the yard, the hoofs of their mounts sending up little puffs of dust. He studied them, his dark eyes taking in the tough exteriors of the two gunmen. Run of the mill gunnies, he thought, using his professional eye to judge them. One was tall and thin, the other heavy and powerfully built. They were both grasping the butts of their holstered guns, and Buck could see that they were straining in their eagerness to get into action. He let his eyes come to the rugged face of the foremost man. This would be Ben Lazzard, he guessed.

The owner of the Lazy L was tall, heavy and tough, a man in his middle forties, and there was much in his rugged face to warn Buck to be careful. Buck had plenty of experience with hardcases, and he could sum them up almost at a glance, and he knew by looking at Ben Lazzard that the rancher would have to be killed before they stopped whatever game he was playing. It was in the man's shoulders, his whole manner, and it stared out of his cold blue eyes.

Lazzard reined up a couple of yards out from the porch, staring from John Larew to Buck, and then back again. The silence was heavy, almost painful, and Buck took an easy breath through his clenched teeth. His dark eyes were narrowed to mere slits, and he had the three men in his gaze. He waited for someone to speak.

"Looks like that brother of yours turned up after all, Larew," Lazzard said suddenly, and his voice was pitched low, thick and insolent. The pale eyes surveyed Buck for a moment, who straightened a little.

"What do you want around here?" Buck demanded.

A grin came to the rugged face, and the leathery cheeks creased for a moment before the muscles relaxed. Then the features became set, and the eyes turned hard and merciless.

"Sounds to me like you've got more guts than your brother. But you ain't got any manners. Come up from Texas, don't you? Mebbe you don't know about the hospitality a man can expect in this county!"

"I know the kind of men who can expect hospitality in any county," Buck replied, "but you don't seem to fit into that category, Lazzard. From what I've heard about you I'd say you're a trouble-maker. Well take a warning as of now. I've spent the last five years handling trouble-makers, and I'm still alive. Now if you've got nothing important on your mind then turn that hoss around and get out of here. Don't come back. There's been some shooting up and attempts at scaring around this place, but I'm telling you that the next gunman who comes around here waving a gun will get a slug for his trouble. That's the way I handle that kind."

"Regular fire-eater, huh?" Ben Lazzard demanded. He was grinning tightly, but there was no mirth in him. "I reckon I better warn my boys to be careful, or you might scare the hell outa them."

"If they're behind this trouble then they better watch out," Buck agreed. "That's all I got to say on it. Now what the hell do you want?"

"You like to put things down on the line," Lazzard

said. "Okay, then I'll do the same. I want this place. My son is getting married in a coupla months, and I figure it'll make a nice wedding present for him. How much you asking for it?"

"It ain't for sale," John Larew snapped, coming forward, and now his face was filled with anger. He was thinking of Letty Haig, and hatred and jealousy made him forget his fear. "You heard what my brother said. Well he's got half shares in this place, and what he says goes. I've taken a lot from your outfit these past weeks, Lazzard, but there's an end to it now. Get to hell out of here and don't show your face around again. We ain't quitting, and we won't take any more threats."

"You figure your brother has got enough spine for the both of you?" the tall gunman demanded.

"Keep your horn out of this," Buck rapped. "Hired men should keep their mouths shut until they're spoken to. Try to act tough around here and you'll go out of this yard face down across your saddle."

John Larew threw a glance at his brother, and saw the change that had come over Buck. His brother had not moved a muscle since the trio rode in, but now there was an intentness in his gaze, a stiffness in his attitude that bespoke of a terrible eagerness to kill. The expressionless manner seemed to communicate itself to the three horsemen, and Ben Lazzard threw a warning glance at his two men.

"There ain't no need to get your back up," he said placatingly. "I rode in here on a peaceful visit. It ain't my fault that you have been getting trouble around the county from someone. Don't try to take it out on us. Find the guilty men and handle them."

"I know who's behind it," John Larew said tightly. "Now enough has been said. We ain't in the market. You better leave, Lazzard."

"Mind if we water our broncs?" Lazzard demanded.

"Just don't try anything else," Buck rapped. He did not move as Lazzard turned his horse away and moved to the watering trough across the yard. The two gunmen sat their horses for a moment, staring at Buck, and then the taller one of the two unclamped his jaws and spoke harshly.

"I'm Stringfinger Dunn, hombre," he snarled. "I don't take kindly to a tongue like yours. Cross my path around this county and I'll call you out."

"If that's the way you feel about it then make your play right now," Buck invited, not moving a muscle. He spoke in even tones, betraying no nervousness or tension, and his soft voice seemed to disconcert the gunman. The silence stretched on for a bit, and then Buck pushed himself away from the post. He set his feet apart and flexed the fingers of his gunhand. "What you waiting for?" he demanded. "If you're gonna wander around looking for a chance to get at me then you might as well do it now. Your nerves might get a bit frayed if you wait too long, and likely you'd toss a slug into my spine. So get to it, Dunn. Draw or get to hell outa here."

The other gunman remained motionless. Both men were tense, ready to start pulling their weapons. John Larew was frozen in the doorway, his face showing agony. He didn't want shooting, and he couldn't understand his brother pushing for it. But Buck had been a Texas Ranger, and he was fast with a gun. Perhaps it would be better to show a strong hand now, and go into this at the outset as they intended going on. They had no intention of pulling out, and if that caused a fight then they had to make a bold stand. The silence dragged on, and the two gunmen did not move.

"Seems to me you've lost your nerve," Buck said finally. "You just turn those hosses around and get out of here, and I'll forget that threat you made just now. But don't ever cross my trail around here again or I'll start smoking my Colt. I don't take to threats, and don't forget it."

Ben Lazzard watered his horse, then realized that his two men were not with him. He turned and yelled for them, and after a long pause Stringfinger Dunn cursed half to himself and wheeled his mount away. He galloped across the yard, followed by the other gunnie, and John Larew let his breath go in a long sigh as the tension eased. The gunmen watered their horses, and then followed Lazzard out of the yard. As they disappeared Johnny Thorne came out of the barn and walked across the yard towards the house, still holding his rifle. Buck turned to his brother, and his face was deadly serious.

"Well we put Lazzard in his place, John," he remarked. "I hope you can see that it had to be done. From what you told me, and from what I saw in Lazzard himself, I'd say we're in for a rough time of it, so we haven't done ourselves any harm by laying it down thick and heavy. Mebbe we've made Lazzard think a bit, but whatever comes up, I ain't gonna be caught napping. I reckon it's a good thing for you that I've shown up now. We'll see just what happens when Lazzard has had a chance to think this over. He knows he's got to fight now if he wants anything around here."

"And that's what worries me," John Larew said tightly.

CHAPTER 2

BEN LAZZARD put his horse into a fast run when he left the Bar Sixty yard, and his two gunmen had to ride hard to keep within touch. But when he was out of sight of the Larew ranch Lazzard reined up and sat his mount, waiting for Dunn and Rod Culley to come up with him. Dunn's leathery face was showing anger when he reined in beside his boss.

"I'll stick behind if you like, Ben," he said tightly. "When that ex-Ranger shows his nose off the place I'll kill him."

"You'll do no such thing, Stringfinger," Lazzard said ferociously. "What the hell do I pay you for? You'll take orders without question. What do you want to do, start a range war around here?"

"What the hell have you been trying to do?" Dunn countered. "We've been hitting each of the ranchers around here. We tore out Wire Sutton's fence and ran off some of his stock. What was that done for?"

"All part of my plan, like Ike's handling Letty Haig. That's the way to get John Larew going. You saw his face when I mentioned that I wanted the Bar Sixty for Ike after his marriage. The old days of shooting the hell out of your neighbours for their range are past, Stringfinger, so start using your sense. We've got to handle this careful, or we'll have the law breathing down our necks."

"That old fool Bub Wickup is just a poor excuse for a lawman," Rod Culley said.

"You're another one," Lazzard said heavily. "None of you have got any sense. Couldn't you see the kind of man Buck Larew is? I spotted it the instant I laid my eyes on him. There ain't many of his breed around, I can tell you, and a good thing too. He's the kind that you can't kill. If I turned the whole outfit out to get him he'd come out on top. He's been a Texas Ranger, and they're a tough outfit. We don't want any trouble with him."

"How you gonna get around him then?" Dunn demanded, staring back in the direction of the Bar Sixty. "When we handle his brother he's gonna step in against us, ain't he? He sure gave me the impression that he would."

"He'll start fighting, but when he does I want it to be on my terms," Lazzard commented. "Come on, let's get back to our place. I want to have a word with Ike. He'd better not go throwing his weight around in Rainbow Creek while Buck Larew is here. Them two Larews are different to each other, and it sticks out a mile."

"You afraid of him?" Dunn asked as they gigged their mounts forward.

"Nope," Lazzard replied, "but I got enough sense to respect a man like him. We're gonna play this smart in future. I want some more pressure put on Wire Sutton. You can run off some more of his stock. Then pay a visit to Whiskey Clanton's place. You know there's been some tension between Clanton and Sutton over that waterhole on their boundary. Well I reckon now is the time someone should poison that water. Clanton claims it, and he'll figure that Sutton poisoned it. Let's keep the pot boiling, huh?"

"It'll be a pleasure," Dunn said. "But I'd still like a crack at that Buck Larew. I didn't like the look of him nohow. He was too sure of himself."

"That should have told you the kind of man he is," Lazzard commented. "But I guess you ain't got no sense, Stringfinger. Just you do like I tell you with no questions asked and this will turn out just how I want it."

Dunn began to argue, but Lazzard pushed his horse into a run and started fast for the Lazy L. The two gunmen followed him closely, and anger was still throbbing through Dunn. He hadn't liked the way Buck Larew had spoken to him, and although he had got some feeling about Larew, an undefinable thrill of cold fear which stabbed through him at Larew's coldly offered challenge to fight, he didn't think he would come out second best in a showdown. He had quite a reputation himself, and his natural hatred for a lawman, or even an ex-lawman, made him underestimate Buck Larew's potential.

Ben Lazzard let his thoughts rove over the broad situation, which was of his own making. He had been stirring up trouble in this country for a long time, and everything had been working according to his schemes. He had most of the ranchers up in arms over the tension and disputes that were growing daily. Lazzard had played his game with deep cunning, and although he was suspected of being at the back of the unrest he knew the difference between suspicion and proof. He was aided by the fact that Sheriff Bub Wickup was not very energetic in his law dealing. But he was aware of the dangers that were attendant to this course he was taking. Now he had seen Buck Larew he realized that those dangers were very much greater. Something would have to be done about the ex-Ranger, and it would have to be done carefully. There would only be one chance, he knew, and guessed that it was a chore he could not delegate to one of his gunmen. They were all right in their own deadly way, but they didn't seem to have the intelligence to plan a quiet coup and make it succeed. Their knowledge did not extend beyond their own capabilities, and they figured that the only way to handle trouble was by facing it and attempting to beat it with gunspeed. That was all right if they were fast enough, but should they come up against a faster man then the whole scheme would suffer, and he had advanced too far in recent months to want to risk failure now through precipitate action.

He was playing for big stakes, and so far he had no complaints about the way things were working out. His son had given him plenty of reason for apprehension, but it seemed that Ike was going to marry Letty Haig, and the girl should have a quietening influence upon the youngster. Lazzard knew now that he had given Ike too much rope in his youth. The youngster had made an unenviable reputation for himself in the county, and it would take some living down; drinking and gambling and rough living. But put him into the Bar Sixty with a wife and there should be great improvement.

Lazzard reined up when he came in sight of his own spread. He grinned tightly at the thought of his own advancement in this county. He had been in occupation about twelve years, and the time had flown since he robbed a bank and got away with enough dough to start his Lazy L. He had named the ranch well, he thought. He had been a lazy man himself, working just to get things going before handing over the reins of the spread to Rowdy Keeler, his able foreman. The Lazy L had grown in the past five years, and mainly on account of Lazzard's handling of his neighbours. He had taken over three smaller spreads after arranging for their owners to be scared enough to sell. He had been working on John Larew for the Bar Sixty, and his pale eyes narrowed when he thought of Buck Larew. There was a fly in the ointment if ever he'd seen one. He would have to handle Buck Larew carefully.

He rode into his yard and dismounted at the porch

of the big house. Ben Lazzard liked his creature comforts, and had spent much on his home. He was proud of the Lazy L, and intended further expansion as more of his plans came to fruition. But money was getting short now, and already he had planned a bank raid which would replenish his dwindled resources. He handed his reins to Stringfinger Dunn, and as the two gunmen moved away he called out to Dunn.

"Look up Drago Heppell and tell him to come on over to the house. I wanta talk to him."

Dunn nodded surlily. No one on the Lazy L liked Drago Heppell, who had ridden with Ben Lazzard in the old days. Lazzard had been making a name for himself in the north-east States before settling down with his spoils. The wild life had appealed to him, and at times even now he felt the pull of the old days. But he had disciplined himself well. He had passed over many chances because he knew that one slip would put him back on the long trail for the rest of his life, and now he was beginning to feel old. His age was catching up on him, and he wanted nothing more than to settle down here on the Lazy L and take things easy.

He stalked into the house and went into his library. The high walls were loaded with books. He had been a great reader in his time, and spent most of his time now with a book in his hands. He went to the large desk and sat down on the leather covered easy chair. He reached for the bottle of whisky and the glass that stood on the tray, and helped himself to a liberal tot. He drank easily, and as he set down the glass the door of the room was thrust open and his son entered.

Ike Lazzard was like his father in many respects. Physically they were almost identical twins, except that Ben showed his age. Ike was tall and heavily built, with the same rugged face and pale blue eyes. Looking at his son, Ben could see much of himself in the youngster, and he wasn't pleased. He had been a profligate himself most of his life, but he'd worked hard when he'd had to, and his cunning brain had helped him get where he was today, but Ike was content to rest upon his father's laurels. The youngster, nearing twenty-one, had all of the vices and none of the desire to work. He had lazed around the county, wasting his youth, spending money like water, and the signs of his shallow life were stamped indelibly upon his face.

"Howdy, Pa," he greeted, moving to a chair and dropping into it. "Heard you ride in. Gimme some dough, will ya? I got to make it to Rainbow Creek now. I promised Letty that I'd drop by and see her."

"You spent out what I gave you yesterday?" Ben Lazzard demanded. "Hell, boy, that stuff don't grow on trees. You should have some respect for dough. Before you die you might realize that it's the best friend a man can have in this world. I ain't got no spare cash on me right now. What I gave you yesterday should have lasted you the month."

"It's an expensive business, preparing to get married," Ike told his father, his heavy face showing a scowl. "I ain't too keen on the idea, you know, and nor is she. You're the one who wants her kept from John Larew. Though why he can't be rubbed out with a gun I don't know."

"You just leave the figuring to me," Ben snapped. He jerked open a drawer and lifted out a heavy metal cash box. He took a bunch of keys from his pocket, selected one and unlocked the box. Ike got to his feet and moved around the desk to take a look inside the box, but Ben took out a wad of notes and slammed down the lid. "Here you are," he commented, peeling half a dozen tens from the wad. "But don't come to me again this side of the end of the month. Is Rowdy back yet with the boys?"

"Got in half an hour ago," Ike said, pocketing the money and moving to the door. "Said everything went off okay. They ripped down some of Sutton's fence, and got away unseen. But I reckon you're wasting your time getting them to play games like that. What you need around here are a couple of killings."

"We might just get some of that if you and the rest of the bunch don't watch your step," Ben said gruffly. "I've come from the Bar Sixty."

"Did Larew offer to sell out?" Ike demanded eagerly.

"Nope, and his brother has showed up. I saw him." Ben's pale eyes glittered at the memory. "Buck Larew is a real tough hombre, and I've seen my share of his kind around. If you come up against him in Rainbow Creek then keep outa his way."

"I ain't backing down from no one," Ike said.

"More fool you then," Ben told him. "You'll get yourself killed."

"I'm riding into town now," his son said. "I'll kill this ex-Ranger for you if I come across him."

"Get outa here, you young fool," Ben Lazzard snapped.

His son grinned and departed, and Ben poured himself another drink. There was a rap at the door and he called out an invitation. The door was thrust open and Drago Heppell entered. Heppell was one of the fastest gunmen Ben Lazzard had ever seen. Heppell was tall and slim, dark haired, and possessing cold brown eyes that had about as much expression in them as a snake's. Heppell had been a gunman from the time he was old enough to carry a gun, and he had ridden with some of the toughest outlaws of the West. The fact that he was still around testified to his skill and cunning.

"You wanta see me, Boss?" Heppell demanded. He had a young-looking face, but there were grey hairs at his temple. He could have been aged anywhere between thirty and fifty. He was a slow talking man with a soft voice, and he never altered expression. But Ben Lazzard knew him for a deliberate killer. They had carried out the last bank raid, and Heppell had killed off the two pards they'd had with them on that occasion. The gunman had settled down on the Lazy L, and hadn't moved far from the spread in the past twelve years, riding into town now and again for some diversion.

"Of course I wanta see you, Drago," Lazzard snapped. "I sent you into Rainbow Creek to weigh up the bank, didn't I?"

"That's right, and I done it," the gunman retorted. He sat down and glanced at the whisky bottle. Lazzard nodded and filled a glass, and held it out to the gunman. Heppell took the drink and tossed it down his throat as if he didn't like the stuff. Then he set the glass carefully on the desk and leaned back in his seat. His dark eyes held Lazzard's gaze. "We can ride in there any time you like and clean it out," he remarked as if talking about the weather. "No worries there. Best time will be between noon and two, I reckon."

"Okay, so we'll pull it off. We're gonna need a couple of strange hosses, and we'll be masked."

"When?" Heppell demanded.

"The sooner the better. I'm getting short of dough. It cost me a lot to take over those three spreads. I don't want to sell any stock just now. We've got to build up, not start selling. So you watch that bank some more and let me know the best day to hit it. We'll handle it alone. The two of us can handle it okay."

"Sure." Heppell got to his feet and started for the

door. He paused with his hand on the doorknob, and glanced back at Lazzard. "It's about time you laid off the rough stuff around here if you intend to make yourself the big auger in the county."

"What the hell are you talking about?" Lazzard demanded. "You trying to tell me how to run my business? Ain't I done okay so far?"

"Mebbe you have, but you're pushing it too hard. Now's the time to lay off and let the men you've been hitting start on each other. They'll do it if you let them, and you can sit back and watch it all. But you keep pushing Sutton and Clanton like you have and they'll turn on you."

"I'll think about that," Lazzard said slowly. "I ain't never known you to be wrong yet, Drago. Mebbe there's something in what you say."

The gunman smiled crookedly and departed, and Lazzard shook his head slowly and thrust out his underlip. Was he getting in out of his depth? Had he been pushing too hard, or too long? It was a delicate situation, he knew, and many men in similar circumstances had made the mistake of going at it too hard. Perhaps the ranchers around here would keep it up if he relaxed his pressure. He knew for a fact that there was talk about the Lazy L being behind the troubles. He thought again of Buck Larew, and knew that he could make a lot of trouble for himself in that quarter. Unless he set Drago Heppell on to the ex-Ranger!

He moistened his lips as he considered it. It would take a man as good as Drago to handle Buck Larew. But would the ex-Ranger's death lead to widespread trouble? He couldn't afford to let matters get out of hand. As Drago had said, he would have to handle it carefully if he wanted to come out on top.

Lazzard got to his feet and went out in search of his

son. He had pushed Ike into courting Letty Haig, but Ike didn't know that his father had put pressure upon the girl. He had threatened to have John Larew killed if she didn't stay away from him. Larew had been about to marry Letty, but that had been stopped. Now Larew was about ready to start shooting when the girl was mentioned. Lazzard knew he had made a bad mistake in not having John Larew killed before his brother showed up. Now it seemed as if he was too late for those tactics. If anything happened to John Larew then Buck would go through the entire county killing off the men he figured were responsible.

Having built up the situation from nothing, with only his cunning to aid him, Ben Lazzard was determined to make his plans succeed. He had the whole county in the palm of his hand. He hadn't hurried things. He had worked quietly, aiming for widespread unrest and suspicion, and now his neighbours were almost at each other's throats. That was what he wanted, and he was about to push them that last fraction to start the trouble, but the situation had changed imperceptibly, and it was only his seeing the kind of man that Buck Larew was that warned him.

He went out into the bright sunlight, narrowing his eyes against the glare. He wouldn't be beaten. Something had to happen to Buck Larew, and quick. But it was a dangerous situation. If he had Buck Larew killed it might stir up the law from its lethargy, and if he left the ex-Ranger alive the man might weigh in against him and come out on top.

Lazzard spotted Ike coming out of the barn, and called to his son. The youngster came across, his heavy face filled with impatience.

"I was on my way out," Ike complained.

"I want you to stick around here now," Ben said

thinly. "There's a crisis, and I don't want you out in the open until it's been settled."

"What the hell!" the youngster bristled. "I'm riding in to see Letty. She ain't too keen on me, you know. She's still got a hankering for John Larew."

Ben Lazzard didn't comment upon that. He was wondering if his threats had been strong enough to persuade the girl to maintain her aloofness from the Bar Sixty. She had realized that John Larew could be shot dead if it was ordered, but Lazzard figured the girl might not have the courage to go through with a marriage to his son. He thinned his lips as he had a moment's intuition. He suddenly saw all his plans cracking and failing. He took a quick breath. He wouldn't let it fail.

"I'm riding into Rainbow Creek," he retorted. "You can ride with me. Saddle up my dun for me. I'll be out in ten minutes. Tell Drago he can ride with us. Send Rowdy in to talk to me."

He went back into the house and changed into clean clothes. When he went down to the porch again Rowdy Keeler was waiting for him. The Lazy L foreman was a tough, massively built man about forty. A craggy face showed all the marks of a hard life. There was a scar on Keeler's left cheek that gave his thin lipped mouth a permanent leer. His brown eyes were narrowed and glittering, too intense, and they warned of his inner fires. Rowdy Keeler had been well nicknamed.

"What do you want, Boss?" Keeler demanded hoarsely.

"You did a good job on Sutton's fence?" Lazzard demanded.

"You don't have to ask, do you?" Keeler replied. "Sure I did. When Sutton finds out about it he'll be hopping mad. I heard talk in town last week that he issued a warning to Clanton. That waterhole business stirred them up."

"Yeah." Lazzard grinned momentarily. "It's easy to put one man against the other, huh? Now I want to get things really moving. You know what the plan is. I want that waterhole poisoned. When Clanton's cows start dying he'll take a gun to Sutton."

"It'll start a range war for sure," Keeler observed.

"But we won't be dragged in," Lazzard said. "We'll wait until the smoke blows away, and then we'll be sitting pretty."

"What about John Larew? You want some more pressure put on him?"

"Nope. Lay off him, and warn the crew to stay away from Buck Larew."

"I heard about him from Stringfinger. He sure rubbed him up the wrong way. Stringfinger is ready to lay for him, if you want some action."

"I already told Dunn to lay off," Lazzard said. "I don't want too much trouble all at once. I don't know what to do about the Larews now. So I'm hanging fire until things clear up a bit. You get on with that waterhole. We could do with some gunsmoke drifting now. It'll give the law something to handle, and I got another iron in the fire that's due to come out any time."

"We ain't got nothing to worry about the law," Keeler said. "You couldn't have a better set-up here, Boss."

"It could be a lot better," Lazzard said. "I'm riding into town now. I'll be gone a couple or three days. Keep a close eye on everything until I get back, and no more trouble. Just do what I've told you."

"You can rely on that, Boss," the foreman said, moving to the door. "Good hunting."

Ben Lazzard grunted and followed Keeler out. He saw his son over at the corral, and Drago Heppell was with

him. They were mounted, and Lazzard's dun was ready
saddled and waiting.

"You changed your mind, Ben?" Heppell demanded.
"You getting impatient?"

"Nope," Lazzard snapped, swinging into his saddle
and gathering up the reins. "But we've got to keep
pushing."

"One of these days you're gonna push too damn hard,"
Ike told him. "I don't know what the hell you're after
around here, Pa, but you're stacking up trouble for the
whole bunch of us."

"You wouldn't have such an easy time of it if I hadn't
schemed most of my life," Lazzard retorted. "You know
damn well what I'm up to, and when I die I've got to
leave it all to you."

"That'll be the day," his son responded.

"Come on, let's raise dust," Lazzard said, and rowelled
his mount cruelly. The animal leaped across the yard in
a series of lunges, and Lazzard set his teeth and rode the
beast straight for the gate. He went out to the range like
a whirlwind, leaving his son and the gunman behind, and
he breathed heavily with the wind in his face, feeling his
pulses leaping and his blood racing. He pushed the dun
for a mile before allowing it to ease, and then he twisted
in his saddle and looked for his companions. They were
three hundred yards behind. He reined up and waited for
them to reach him.

"You're gonna kill that hoss one day," Ike Lazzard
reproved.

"I got plenty more back there," Ben retorted. "Come
on, let's get moving. It's a helluva way into Rainbow
Creek."

"Get there about ten tonight," Drago Heppell commented.

They maintained a good pace, and the afternoon wore

away and evening brought its cooling breeze. The sky was dappled with light cloud, and the slanting rays of the sun brought out the slinking shadows that soon began to darken and cover the low places, They rode in silence, each lost in his thoughts, but as the sun went Ben Lazzard straightened in his saddle and glanced around.

"When we hit town, Ike," he said, "you go along to see Letty and ask her to come spend a few days out at the ranch. Until I can get hold of the Bar Sixty you're gonna have to live at the Lazy L, and you better get that gal in the mind to do some cleaning and preparing out there. We'll soon see how enthusiastic she is about the whole idea."

"I've got the feeling that she'll get cold feet before the day," Ike said, and Drago Heppell laughed harshly.

"What's on your mind?" Ben Lazzard snarled.

"I'd think twice before I'd marry into your family, Ben," Heppell said, and Ike cursed him heavily.

They continued along the broad trail, and topped a rise and saw the town of Rainbow Creek spread out before them. There was a wide expanse of glinting water beyond the town, and the last rays of the sun were touching its rippled surface.

"I'm gonna make a lot of changes around here when I get control," Ben said.

"That'll be the day," Ike told him. "You don't think these folk will stand for you taking over like that, do you?"

"You just shut your mouth about things you don't know," his father told him. "Get on down there and tell that gal what she's got to do. I'll see you at the hotel later, and don't get into any trouble. We're sticking around here tomorrow, and we'll probably ride for home the day after."

Ike grinned and spurred his horse down the slope, and Ben watched his son for some moments before he glanced at Heppell. The gunman was staring down the slope, the last of the sun lighting his craggy face. His eyes were filled with strange fire, and for a moment Lazzard stared at Heppell, fascinated by the bleakness, the naked death that shone out of the craggy features.

"Drago, we're gonna hit that bank tomorrow," Lazzard said.

"Okay," the gunman responded. "About half-twelve would be the best time."

"We'll pick up a couple of spare hosses early in the morning. Think you can handle that? I've had the plan in my mind for a long time, so we don't have to worry about that. The hosses will be left at the back of the bank. We'll go in through the front door, lock it, and then beat it out the back way when we've got the loot. If there's no shooting then we shouldn't have any trouble."

"It'll work," Heppell said. "But we'll have to change our clothes after or we'll be recognised."

"You think I'm some kind of a sucker?" Lazzard demanded, grinning. "I've got a cabin on the edge of town. Bought it last year, although I ain't never used it. But I figured it might come in handy some day. I've got plenty of spare clothes there. We'll dress ourselves just before the raid, and cross the back lots to the alley beside the bank. You can get the horses in that derelict barn just back of the bank. We'll sneak into the bank, lift the dough, and make it away clean as a whistle."

"Sounds okay," Heppell said. "The bank should be deserted by the time we walk in. How you gonna cut up the dough?"

"You can leave your share in with mine and we'll play it together for these other ranches after the shooting has started," Lazzard said. "But that's up to you, Drago. You know your own mind, huh?"

"Yeah. I'll have cold cash," the gunman retorted. "I don't want anything to do with your schemes, Ben. If we have to get out fast I'll have cash in hand. You'll lose everything if you have to quit. You won't get the chance to sell out."

"I ain't that kind of a man," Ben Lazzard snapped, his jaw clenching. "I ain't gonna back down from anything. If this turns sour on me I'm gonna stand my ground and shoot it out. They'll have to kill me to finish me."

"That's a fool's way of talking and you know it," Heppell said. "But it's your life, Ben. You do as you please."

"I always have," the big rancher said, smiling grimly. "I don't intend to change now. You'll see that this will work out, Drago. I always come out on top."

"There's a first time for everything," the gunman replied. "You'll come a cropper one of these days, and no mistake, and it'll likely be for something big. You'll be the talk around here for years, after you're gone."

"Now you're scaring me," Ben Lazzard retorted, grinning. "Come on, let's get into town and take a look around. I want to check the approaches to the bank. We're gonna ride out of town, and then cut back. We'll dump the dough in my cabin and then show ourselves around town. Then tomorrow we'll pick up the dough and take it out to the ranch."

"Sounds all right." Heppell pushed his mount forward and they continued towards Rainbow Creek. The gunman let his thoughts roam over the plan, and could not fault it. They needed a simple operation, and with the law in such a poor state around here there wasn't much chance of things going wrong.

Ben Lazzard was grinning as they rode into the sprawling town. The money in the bank was as good as his, and he'd kill if he had to, just to make it so. Nothing was going to stop him.

CHAPTER 3

BUCK LAREW felt restless as evening drew on. He had eaten, and was sitting on the porch beside his brother. The sun was low in the sky, but he had no eyes for the beauty of the sunset. He kept staring at John's impassive face, taking in the signs of strain that showed. His brother looked ten years older than his age, and in the old days John Larew had been a carefree man.

"I reckon we should get to work at once on this business, John," he said suddenly, and startled his brother from his deep thoughts. John Larew glanced at him, frowning.

"What do you mean, Buck? You want to take the fight to the Lazzards?"

"Safest way of handling the business. I know what I'm talking about. Ben Lazzard is a mighty determined man. Whatever he's planned will be done, never fear, and when he does strike you can bet that we won't get any kind of a chance. They've already put a slug into you from ambush."

"That was done as a warning," John Larew said.

"But the next time it might be for keeps." Buck narrowed his eyes as he stared out into space. "Let's get prepared for trouble. That way we'll have a chance of surviving."

"I don't think it will come to that if we lay off," John said doggedly. "It's your experience riding for the law that makes you want to start shooting Buck. But I don't want to start anything. We'd have the law on us if we began the shooting."

"Let's go have a talk with Wire Sutton. He seemed

a determined man to me, and he's sure got something to kick up about. They ripped down his fence this afternoon. I saw the half dozen riders making off."

"Were you close enough to see them in detail?"

"Nope. That was a pity. If I had we'd be able to go to the law and get something done. But Sutton is convinced that the Lazzards organised it. There was some lead slinging, but Sutton didn't recognise any of the riders."

John Larew sighed. He got to his feet and started pacing the porch. Buck watched him for a time, then got up. He moved to the edge of the porch and leaned against a post. Johnny Thorne was coming out of the barn, and the young cowboy peered around then came across the yard. When he reached the bottom step of the porch John Larew turned to him.

"Johnny, saddle up a couple of horses, will you? I'm gonna take a ride across to the Broken S. Buck will come with me. You keep your eyes open until we get back, just in case."

"Sure." The cowboy turned and went across the yard.

John turned to Buck, and for a moment they stared at each other. The reddened rays of the sun made John Larew's face crimson, and the determination that showed on his features looked like a dull stain.

"What have you decided?" Buck demanded.

"We're gonna fight," his brother retorted thickly. "What the hell! I've let the Lazzards do just as they like around me. Ike has taken my girl, and Ben has been putting the fear of God into me. But that's ended. Come on, let's ride across to see Sutton. If we've got to fight then we'll do it willingly, and on our own terms. Like you say, if we lay off and let the Lazzards make the first move we'll be at a disadvantage."

"Now you're talking," Buck said. He drew his Colt,

checked the weapon, and slid it back into its holster. "We'll give them something to think about."

"You better handle the deal," John said. "You've been a lawman, and you know about this sort of thing. What's our first move?"

"We've got to get proof that the Lazzards are breaking the law," Buck replied. "Don't think that we're gonna ride over to the Lazy L and shoot the hell out of them. That's not the way to handle it. That's the kind of thing Ben Lazzard is expecting, and you can bet that he's got his crew on their toes for just such an act. We'd get shot to pieces if we tried that. The only thing to do, as I see it, is get some proof against the Lazy L, and present it to the law."

"But I've told you that the law is useless around here," John Larew protested.

"I reckon I can shake it up to do what we want," Buck promised. "Sutton's foreman, Foster, said that the deputy ain't a bad hombre. We'll get him to take a party of us along to the Lazy L when we've got our proof."

"That might work, but I doubt if the sheriff would deputise anyone for a chore like that."

"He'd have to do something if there was proof placed before him," Buck insisted. "Don't start crossing rivers before you come to them, John. Let's go have a talk with Sutton. He seemed mighty determined to have a go when he left me."

"Okay. I'm all for it now. I've been holding off because I figured this place ain't worth dying for, but I've been wrong, Buck. A man has a duty to protect what belongs to him in this world. We'll do what we have to."

Johnny Thorne came back across the yard leading two horses, and Buck and his brother stepped down off the porch. The cowboy handed over their reins and they both mounted. John Larew stared down at Thorne.

"Don't take any chances around here, Johnny," he commanded. "If there is any trouble while we are away then you cut and run. You can always come back later."

"Not me," the cowboy asserted. "If trouble hits while I'm alone you can bet that I'll face it out. No one is gonna run me out."

"Thanks. See you when we get back." John Larew glanced at the sober faced Buck, and they started across the yard. "I'm thinking that after the reception Lazzard got here this afternoon he might shake up his ideas about giving me some trouble."

"You're not alone now," Buck replied. "I'm around, and anyone riding in here to throw lead around is gonna get some back, and quick. I don't think Lazzard will handle it like that, though. He's gonna figure that he'll get some trouble if his boys wage war openly. I think we're gonna have to watch out for fence cutting and ambushing."

"They already tried ambushing," John said uneasily, gazing around into the encroaching shadows.

"It's a nasty business, but now you're on your guard it shouldn't go too badly. If Sutton is still determined to fight then we'll get somewhere. How far is it to his place?"

"About six miles from here," John Larew retorted. He put his horse into a run and Buck kept beside him as they crossed the range. Night fell and darkness closed in around them, but John Larew knew where he was going, and maintained a fast pace. The dark miles dropped behind, and when they breasted a rise Buck spotted light in the distance. "The Broken S," John Larew commented.

They rode into the ranch boldly, fearing that Sutton might have put his outfit on their guard, and some cowboys were notoriously trigger-happy. As they moved slowly across the yard a harsh voice challenged them.

"Hold it and declare yourselves."

"John Larew and his brother."

"Okay, come on in."

They rode to the front of the house and dismounted. A figure appeared from the shadows and advanced towards them, a rifle covering them, and then the man grunted his satisfaction and turned away.

"Is Wire about?" John Larew demanded.

"Sure, he's in the house."

They stepped on to the porch, and as John Larew reached out to knock on the door it was jerked open. The bulky figure of Wire Sutton appeared.

"Howdy, John," the rancher greeted. "Glad to see you. But what brings you over here at this time? Not fresh trouble, is it? I told Buck I'd drop in and talk with you tomorrow morning."

"No trouble yet, Wire," John Larew replied, "but we figure that we oughta prepare for anything."

"My sentiments," the rancher replied. "Come on in. I've got Rake Foster inside. We've been discussing plans. After what happened to my fence today I've got to do something. These terrorising raids are getting worse and worse. The next thing to happen will be bloodshed, and I mean to get in first."

The brothers entered the house and followed Sutton into a room on the left of the wide passage that cut through the house. Rake Foster got to his feet, grinning his pleasure, and Buck, studying the Broken S foreman, decided that if the rest of Sutton's crew were as tough and capable as this man looked then they would hold their own against the Lazy L.

"Sit down, the both of you," Sutton invited. "Drink?"

"No thanks," John Larew said. He sat down in a seat that was in the far corner.

Buck nodded when Sutton caught his eye and raised a whisky bottle, and he took a tall glass that was half filled with spirit and moved to a chair by the window and sat down. He glanced at the window and saw that the blind was drawn, and he got up and moved his chair slightly so his shadow was not thrown on the blind. Then he relaxed.

"What's happened to make you change your mind about fighting?" Sutton demanded.

John Larew told the rancher about Lazzard's visit to the Bar Sixty. Sutton nodded when he had finished, and sighed heavily.

"Things are beginning to move and no mistake," he commented. He glanced at Buck Larew. "But you told Lazzard in no uncertain terms about what he could expect. Do you expect him to take you up on that?"

"I don't know him well enough to hazard even a guess," Buck replied. "But I'll tell you what I've got in mind, shall I?"

"Please do." Sutton poured himself a drink and leaned back in his seat.

"It'll be asking for trouble to gather what men you have and ride across to the Lazy L and shoot it out with them," Buck went on. "I figure that Lazzard will be expecting that. What we've got to do is have a couple of men watching the Lazy L all the time and check upon the movements of Lazzard's crew. If any of them ride out to raise hell then we'll know about it, and with proof we can demand protection from the law."

"You'll be wasting your time riding into Rainbow Creek for help," Rake Foster said. "The law ain't on our side."

"That's what I told him," John Larew said. "But he will have that we can make the law do what we want if we get proof."

"Sure we can," Buck said. "I ain't concerned with that part of it. But how do you feel about playing a waiting game?"

"I'll ride in with the idea," Sutton said. "It was the line I was taking with Rake here. I figure that it would be plumb foolish to attack the Lazzards. They're too strong for us, but I didn't intend riding into town for help when I got my proof. I would have staged an ambush for the Lazy L and shot them to bits."

"What we do about them after we've got proof will depend upon what they do when they give us the proof," Buck said. "Having been a lawman I'd prefer to work within the law, and that would be the safest bet. But if it gets real rough then we'll handle it ourselves."

"I'm thinking that you'd better go into Rainbow Creek and take a look at the local law department," Rake Foster said. "You'll get a surprise, Buck."

"We can ginger them up if they need it. How many men you got will carry a gun for you?"

"I got five riders on my payroll," Sutton said. "With me and Rake that's seven."

"And me and John make it nine," Buck mused. "How many men has Ben Lazzard got at his call?"

"Say twice as many," Foster retorted. "That's odds of two to one in their favour, and they're all tough gun-hands, you can bet."

"Not too bad, so long as we meet them on our terms," Buck said, smiling thinly. "Okay, so we're agreed, are we? We'll watch the Lazzards and try to catch them red handed pulling some of their tricks. If we do get the goods on them we'll send for the law."

"And if the law don't give us any satisfaction then we'll handle it ourselves," Sutton ended.

"That's right." Buck glanced at his brother, half expecting some protest, but John Larew merely nodded.

"Then I figure that we better get started with our watching tactics. I'll go along with one of your men for tonight, Wire. I don't know the country, but the sooner I find out where the different places are the better. I'll take watch until dawn, and you can send a couple of men to relieve us. You know the area, so you better name the rendezvous."

"I'll get one of the boys over," Foster said, climbing to his feet. "We're gonna keep a twenty-four hours a day watch on the Lazy L, huh?"

"That's it," Buck said. "If we'd been watching today we would have seen that bunch ride out who tore down your fence."

"I wish I could have caught them," Sutton said grimly. "Yeah, Buck, we'll go through with this. And I reckon you won't have to watch long to nail some of them polecats."

"I might as well head back for home then," John Larew said. "I don't want to leave Johnny long on his own. There's no telling what might start, and if anything happened to him while he was at the spread alone I'd never forgive myself."

"I'll be back some time in the morning," Buck told his brother.

"I've decided to ride into town first thing," John said. "I got some personal business to attend to."

"Wait for me to show up, or better still, come on here and pick me up," Buck said. "It's on the way to town. I'll come in here tomorrow when I get off watch, and we'll head for town. I want to take a look around, and mebbe have a word with the local law."

"That's settled them." Rake Foster went out of the room, and John Larew got to his feet.

"Be careful tonight, Buck," his brother told him. "Don't take any chances."

"We ain't gonna do a blamed thing," Buck retorted. "All we're doing is watching for trouble. It's a safe bet."

"Nothing's safe while there are men like the Lazzards around," John Larew said. "I'll be here just after sunup, Buck."

"See you then," Buck responded. "Watch your step on the way home."

John Larew went out, and when the door had closed behind him Sutton turned to Buck.

"He's taken a lot from the Lazy L lately," the rancher said. "I think he's done well to bear up like he has."

"The Lazy L won't get things all their own way in future," Buck promised.

Foster came back with a tall, thin cowboy following. The cowboy had a long face that was thin and pinched around the mouth. His brown eyes were hard and steady, and they studied Buck Larew as Sutton made the introduction.

"Buck, this is Roan Morrell, one of my best men. He'll back you to the hilt, and if there's any shooting at any time you won't have to worry about Roan. He'll stick by you. Roan, this is Buck Larew, John's brother. We're gonna work with him in an attempt to get the better of the Lazzards."

"Howdy, Larew," Morrell greeted. "Glad to know you. It's about time something was done about that bunch who ride for the Lazy L. They've been stalking around the county for too long, throwing their weight about. I'm your man, and you don't have to worry about your back if shooting starts."

"Glad to hear it," Buck replied. "But we don't want any shooting to start with. We'll save that for when the time is right, and then we'll hand out a beating."

"That's what I like to hear," Sutton said, grinning. "Okay, so it's up to you now, Buck. You'll head out now with Roan, and at dawn I'll have two of the others come out to relieve you. Roan, you know your way around the range. Get into a position where you can watch Lazzard's place without being seen yourself. At dawn sneak out and I'll have your relief on hand."

"If anyone leaves the ranch at all during the night we'll follow them," Buck said. "Warn the relief to take over even if they don't see us."

"Okay." Sutton motioned to the whisky. "Want a drink before you go?"

"No thanks," Buck said, smiling. He moved to the door. "If you're ready, Roan, we'll make a start. We might not have any luck. But we can use patience. I'm damn sure something will happen before very long."

They went out into the darkness and climbed into their saddles. Buck lifted a hand to the figure of the rancher standing in the open doorway, and Sutton called out his goodbye. The Broken S cowboy gigged his mount across the yard and Buck followed him. They soon left the ranch, and the darkness of the range closed in about them. Buck shivered in the chill breeze that had sprung up, and he pushed his horse into a lope to keep up with Morrell. The cowboy maintained a fast pace, and Buck was content to follow.

Two hours of riding through the night brought them into rough country, and soon Morrell was slowing the pace. Then the cowboy halted, and Buck rode in close beside him.

"We ain't far from the Lazy L now," Morrell said. "We better leave our broncs here and finish it on foot. I know the spot where we can lay up. We'll be able to see anyone leaving, or hear them, come to that, and our hosses won't be too far away if we need them."

"Okay. I leave it to you," Buck said. "You know your way around here."

They dismounted and tethered their mounts. Morrell started through the shadows, and Buck dropped a hand to the butt of his Colt before following. They moved forward stealthily, and then Morrell dropped to ground, and Buck followed suit. He crawled forward beside the cowboy, and found himself staring down a slope at three lighted windows in a long, squat building.

"Lazzard's bunkhouse," Morrell said. "What you want to do now, sneak in close and hear what they're saying."

"That's an idea," Buck replied slowly, "but it wouldn't do for the pair of us to go in. I'll take a shot at it if you like, while you stick here in case anyone rides out kind of sudden. We don't want to make a mess of this."

"Okay." Morrell didn't hesitate. "You've been a lawman, and you should be used to sneaking around and doing this kind of thing."

"You can say that again," Buck declared, grinning. "Watch out for me coming back. I don't know how long I'll be."

"Take it easy," the cowboy responded.

Buck nodded grimly and started away. He went down the slope in a crouching run, sticking to the shadows, and when he reached level ground he was only a couple of dozen yards from the bunkhouse. He tried not to look at the lighted windows. The surrounding darkness seemed twice as impenetrable when he glanced around, and he slowed his pace and sneaked in close to the back wall of the low building.

When he was pressed against the rough wall he straightened and began to edge in close to a window. He risked a peep inside the bunkhouse, and saw half a dozen men; some lying on their bunks and four of them seated at a long table, playing cards. He could hear the mumble of their voices, but was not able to make out what was being said. He eased back, afraid that his face would be spotted. It seemed that he had wasted his efforts. He couldn't hear a thing. He moved on to another window, and this time the voices came clearly to him. He looked up and saw that the window was open. He pressed closer and listened.

There was a lot of talking, and the harsh voices were not pleasant. The four men at the table were cursing the run of the cards. Two others were seated by the big stove, heads together and mouths working. They looked a tough bunch, Buck decided, and hung on in the hope of hearing something worthwhile, but nothing came out. He began to feel the chill wind cutting through his clothes, and had decided to move back to where Morrell was waiting when he heard the sound of approaching hoofs. He froze in his position and waited tensely.

The hoofs came closer, and he guessed they were crossing the big yard. Three mounts, he figured expertly, and took a quick breath. Minutes passed and impatience began to flare through him. Then the door of the bunkhouse was thrust open and three men entered. Buck stared at them, and recognised one as Stringfinger Dunn. The other two were strangers to him.

The men in the bunkhouse looked up eagerly at the entrance of these three, and one of the card players spoke quickly.

"How'd it go, Rowdy?"

"Okay," the biggest of the three newcomers said hoarsely. He laughed harshly, his fleshy face creasing like old leather. "I'd like to see Whisky Clanton's face when he sees his cattle dying off like flies. We put enough poison in that waterhole to kill all the steers in Kansas."

"There'll be hell to pay tomorrow," Stringfinger Dunn said spitefully, and there was a malicious expression upon his expansive face. "I reckon Clanton will gather up his boys and go for Sutton baldheaded."

"That's the idea of it," Rowdy Keeler said impatiently. "Okay, you fellers, it'll be a hard day tomorrow, and for several days to come. Better get some sleep while you can."

"The boss has gone into town with Ike and Drago," one of the others said. "He ain't coming back for a couple of days. What do you reckon he's planning now?"

"You'll be told when there's some action to handle," Keeler snapped. "Don't ask questions. It ain't healthy around here."

Buck waited it out, but nothing else transpired. He suppressed a shiver and moved away from the building. He stared around as he left the ranch, but saw no sign of a guard. When he was well out of earshot he straightened and started running, and he was breathless when a low voice challenged him near to the spot where he had left Roan Morrell. He replied with his name, and the next moment he was dropping into cover beside the Broken S cowboy.

"Well, Buck?" Morrell demanded.

"Let me get my breath back," Buck retorted. "I sure learned something that'll set you on your ear." He quickly explained to the cowboy what he had heard.

"What the hell!" Morrell jerked up. "That's what we've been waiting for. It'll mean the start of the war that we've been expecting. Those Lazzards are dirty skunks to pull a thing like this."

"We can get something done that'll foil the whole dirty plan," Buck said. "You know where the Clanton place is, don't you?"

"Sure I do."

"Then let's get there and warn Clanton about the waterhole. He can put some men there to keep the cattle away, and in the morning his outfit and yours can get together and take a crack at the Lazy L. I heard that the Lazzards have gone into town for a few days. It will be easy to tackle them there and get the whole thing sorted out before the rest of their outfit can join in."

"You've got the rights of it," Morrell said, getting to his feet. "Come on, we'll make for the Clanton place. Now I know why there's been trouble brewing between us and the Circle C. Lazzard has been stirring in the background. There's been some things happen around here that we knew we didn't do, and Clanton has denied that he knew anything about it. But we'll have to move fast, Buck."

"I'm your man," Buck replied. "Let's get into our saddles and moving."

They went through the shadows and found their horses, moments later were riding fast on a wide detour of the Lazy L. They pushed on as fast as they dared through the darkness, and Buck began to reason out the next moves. If they could get Clanton and his outfit on their side then they would have a strong hand against the Lazy L. It was obvious now that the Lazzards had every intention of making real trouble. Ben Lazzard had shown his hand as far as the Bar Sixty was concerned. He wanted the place for his son Ike. Now he had poisoned a waterhole to start fighting between Clanton and Sutton. This had to be stopped quickly, before violence flared out and engulfed the whole county.

Buck had no idea where they were riding, but he kept beside Morrell as the cowboy hammered on through the darkness. After what seemed an age they began to slow, and then Morrell was reining up.

"The Clanton place is just ahead," he said tightly. "I reckon we'll have to be mighty careful around here. Clanton has threatened to shoot any of our outfit on sight if he catches them on his range."

"This is different," Buck retorted. "We're bringing a

warning to Clanton. He'll soon realize that the Broken S
is on his side."

"His crew will shoot first and ask questions afterwards," Morrell said. "But let's get in there. If we can
prevent any of his cattle from drinking that poisoned
water so much the better. Clanton is a man of quick
temper, and he'll fly off the handle so fast he won't have
time to take in the significance of what's happening. He'll
go off half-cocked."

"Not while I'm around," Buck said. "There won't be
any trouble. Lazzard made a big mistake tonight. We've
got him cold, and I ain't gonna lose the advantage."

They went on more slowly, and Buck soon saw the
dark outlines of a building. Then he spotted a barn, and
a bunkhouse. They reached a gate set in a wooden
fence, and Morrell leaned down to open it. As they
passed through a harsh voice called a challenge to them.

"Hold it right there and declare yourselves."

"Roan Morrell," the cowboy replied instantly. "Want
to have a talk to Clanton."

"What the hell are you doing here, Morrell? You
know we don't allow Broken S skunks on our range."

"I'm Buck Larew, brother of John Larew of the Bar
Sixty," Buck interposed. "This is important. Where's
Clanton?"

"Over here," a harsh voice yelled from the shadows
around the house. "Come on over, but if this is some
more of Sutton's trickery there'll be hell to pay."

Buck started his horse across the yard, and Morrell
kept at his side. The gate swung shut behind them,
and a shapeless figure appeared from the darkness and
walked behind them. Lamplight from one of the windows in the bunkhouse glinted on a weapon in the man's
hands. They reached the house and stepped to the
ground. Morrell remained with the horses, and Buck

stepped on to the porch and faced the tall figure that
appeared. There was a rifle in the rancher's hands.

"You must be Buck Larew," Clanton said thickly.
"Heard you was coming up from Texas. Been a lawman,
ain't you?"

" That's right, and already I've got a slant on the
trouble that's bubbling in this county," Buck replied.
"Pin back your ears and get a load of what I've got to
tell you." He began to give the rancher a brief account
of what had happened, and long before he was through
Clanton was cursing angrily. When Buck fell silent the
rancher stepped to the edge of the sidewalk and shouted
to the guard.

"Hank, turn out the crew. We've got some fast riding
to do, and there'll be shooting at the end of it."

"Hold your hosses," Buck warned. "Let me tell you
the best way to handle this."

"I know the best way," Clanton snapped. "Shooting is
the only language that bunch on the Lazy L will understand. Now I know they're at the back of this I can get
something done. To think that Ben Lazzard has been
coming over here regularly these past weeks, sympathising
with me on account of the trouble I've been getting from
Sutton's outfit, and all the time it's been the Lazy L
raising the ruckus."

"That's right," Buck agreed, "and you'll be playing
right into Lazzard's hands by hitting his place. He's got
some tough gunmen on his payroll, and they're ready for
something like this. You and your boys will get shot to
hell and gone. Your best bet is to try and play it smart.
You've got some allies now."

"The Broken S?" Clanton shook his head. "Me and
Sutton ain't been seeing eye to eye for a long time. We
ain't friends."

"Sutton will be ready to co-operate with you when he

hears what's been going on," Buck said. "I'm heading there right now. Morrell is with me, and he knows what's happened. You better get some men to that waterhole and fence it off so the cattle can't get at the water. And be careful. Lazzard might have arranged for a couple of his men to watch the water to see what happens. If you find anyone skulking around there take him prisoner. But no rough stuff. We've got to get the law in on this. Be at Sutton's place at dawn. My brother will be showing up then, and we can all ride into town. I heard that the two Lazzards and one of their gunmen are in town now, and they plan to stay there for a couple of days. It'll be our big chance to grab them while their outfit ain't around. We'll stick them in jail for what they've done."

"I don't like the idea of bringing the law into it. The sheriff in this county ain't a strong figure. Lazzard would walk outa that jail ten minutes after you turned your back on it. I'm all for fighting. My outfit is plenty tough. We can hit the Lazy L tonight and finish off that bunch of gunmen. Then we'll go on to town and take the Lazzards. I'll finish this trouble once and for all."

"Don't be a damn fool, Clanton," Morrell called out of the darkness. "Can't you see that Larew is talking sense? Join up with us and we'll do this right. If you make a mistake around Lazzard's bunch you'll wind up dead, and your outfit with you."

"Okay," Clanton said after some deliberation. "I'll get some of my boys down to that waterhole and fence it off. Then the whole bunch of us will show up and ride with the Broken S to Rainbow Creek. I just hope this ain't some kind of a joke, or a sneaky trick on the part of Sutton. If I walk into anything I shan't stop shooting until the whole thing is down in the dust."

"Save your shooting for the Lazy L," Buck said thinly.

"You can bet that if we get the Lazzards into jail the Lazy L crew will try to spring them loose."

"Good," Clanton said. "That'll give us the chance to wipe them out."

"We'll be riding then," Buck said. "We're heading back for the Broken S. See you at dawn, Clanton, and keep a curb on your actions until we've decided to handle this the smart way."

"You can rely on me," the rancher said heavily. "And thanks for coming in here, Morrell."

Buck sighed his relief when he was back in his saddle. He and Morrell rode out of the Circle C, and there was a bunch of cowboys moving around the corral, catching their mounts and saddling up. Buck was well pleased now. He stifled his tiredness as they rode on. It was going to be a long night. . . .

CHAPTER 4

BEN LAZZARD rode into the stable in town and stepped heavily from the saddle. He stared around, squinting his eyes against the gloom that hugged the corners of the rambling building. He had always been afraid of getting ambushed. He was not a coward, and would take on any odds in a straight fight, but he couldn't bear the thought of getting a slug from cover. He liked to see what he was fighting, and he squared his shoulders as he led his horse into an empty stall and began to strip off its gear. Drago Heppell beat him to it, and the gunman was standing by, waiting for him by the time he had forked straw into the stall.

"Let's go get a drink," the gunman said. "I'm dry."

"Sure thing. I ain't gonna do much around here. I wanta have a word with Pete Roscoe. Keep your eyes open for him."

"You want someone killed?" Heppell demanded. "I'm your man for that kind of a chore, and don't you forget it."

"Sure, Drago, but this ain't a straightforward killing job, and I don't want to run the risk of it being tracked back to anyone in my outfit. You know there's gonna be a lot of trouble at the Broken S tomorrow when Clanton shows up there with his outfit. Well I want a man like Pete Roscoe on hand to help out with the shooting. Clanton might just talk, although I doubt that, but I got to be ready for anything, and Pete can help things along with a couple of well placed shots."

"Good idea," Heppell commented as they left the

stable. "If all this happens early, so Clanton or Sutton can send into town here for the law, we'll have an easier time of it here ourselves."

"Yeah, we'll watch around in the morning for riders coming in for the law. If everything goes like I've planned we'll never have an easier job than robbing this bank."

They entered the Longhorn Saloon and pushed to the bar. There was a crowd of men inside the saloon, and those at the bar made room for Ben Lazzard. Heppell kept glancing around, staring over his shoulder, a habit of his when in company, and his right hand was down on the butt of his Colt. Lazzard ordered two beers, and he emptied his glass, when it came, without a pause. Then he smacked his lips and wiped his mouth on one sleeve. He looked around the saloon, searching for faces that he knew. He had no friends. He was not that kind of a man. But he had acquaintances, and he nodded to some of them when he caught their eye. He liked to keep in with most of them, for he didn't know what he might want in future.

But he was in no mood for the noise of the saloon, and when Heppell had finished his beer, Lazzard motioned to the door. He hadn't seen Pete Roscoe around, and he didn't want to ask for the man by name. There were some details of his movements that he wanted kept secret. Out on the sidewalk he fumbled in his pocket for some money, and checked that he had sufficient on him to pay for the job he had in mind.

"You go on to the hotel, Drago," he said. "Get me a room. I'll be along later. Wait up for me in case I have anything to talk about."

"Okay." Heppell moved off along the sidewalk and vanished into the shadows.

Lazzard stared around before walking along the street. There was plenty of shadow, and he liked that. He knew where Pete Roscoe lived with some woman, and had determined to visit the small-time crook. But he didn't want to be seen in the area. He walked slowly along the boardwalk, pausing frequently to look around, and his heart gave a great leap when he halted in the mouth of an alley and a voice spoke up from behind him. He whirled quickly, his gunhand moving fast, and he palmed his .45 and stuck the muzzle into the belly of the man who came forward. There was a harsh cackle, and then the sheriff spoke.

"I reckon you're a high strung man, Ben," Bub Wickup said. His face was just a blur in the shadows. He was a small man, though robustly built. The top of his head reached just past Lazzard's shoulder. There was a glint of the law badge pinned to his chest.

"Hell, Bub, you didn't oughta surprise a man that-away," Lazzard said mildly. "I nearly pulled this trigger. The trouble that's springing up around here, you could get yourself shot doing a fool thing like that."

"I didn't do a blamed thing," the little lawman retorted. "I was just standing in here minding my own business when you snaked in. What you playing at, moving around like that?"

"Thought I was being followed by someone out for mischief," Lazzard lied. "I got one or two enemies in this part of the world you know."

"I wouldn't agree to that," Wickup said easily. "You keep yourself to yourself. You ain't like Sutton or that fool Clanton. I guess there will be trouble between them before they get satisfied. I never saw a pair like them. There's enough water in that hole on their boundary to keep both their herds happy, with enough over to drown this town. But they got to keep niggling at each other about it. I guess it'll end up with one or the other of them getting killed. Then they'll be really satisfied."

Lazzard smiled to himself, thinking about the water-hole. By now it should have been salted well with poison, and there surely would be trouble when Clanton found his steers dropped dead around the water.

"You're right, Bub," he said. "Me, I find that ranching is a full-time job. I wouldn't have any time to spare for helling around. I'm allus too tired for anything else when I get my daily chores done."

"Shows the difference there is between a good rancher and the kind that Sutton and Clanton are," Wickup retorted. "I ain't got no time for the likes of them. They keep prodding at each other, and then when there's trouble they yell for help from the law."

Lazzard grinned again. Fat lot of help they'd get from Wickup, he thought. He stepped impatiently out of the alley.

"I'll see you around, Bub," he remarked. "Just gonna get a breath of air before I turn in. I'm staying the night. Will ride back to the Lazy L tomorrow morning."

"So long, Ben," the sheriff replied. "I wish the rest of the ranchers were like you."

Lazzard was grinning tightly as he went on along the street. This county was bad enough with just one like him around. He hated to think what it would have been like with some more of his calibre. He stepped into another alley farther along the street, and nodded to him-self when he spotted the sheriff walking along the side-walk in the opposite direction. Just so long as there were no snoopers watching him, he thought. He went on, moving cautiously, checking his surroundings frequently.

He came to the poorer part of the town, where he had his own cabin, and slipped silently among the small buildings crowded together on the flats south of main street. He kicked at a dog that came growling and snarling out of the darkness, and the animal retreated with a series of yelps. Lazzard thinned his lips and cursed the dog. He kept moving, and found his way through the shadows to a cabin standing on the outskirts of the slum. There was a light in the window, and he kept in the darkness as he rapped on the door.

A woman appeared in reply to his summons, and he averted his face as he spoke.

"Is Pete Roscoe in?" he demanded.

"Sure. You better come in."

Lazzard wrinkled his nose at the stale smells that greeted him as he stepped over the threshold. He looked around the big room with distaste on his rugged features. There was no sign of Roscoe, and he glanced enquiringly at the woman.

"He's in bed," she said. "Ain't been well."

"Too much to drink again?" Lazzard demanded.

"Had pains in the belly," she replied. "You better come through here." She led the way into a smaller room that was bare except for a dirty looking bed and a couple of chairs.

Lazzard breathed shallowly through his nose as he stared at the figure of the man in the bed. A lamp was turned up high, and was smoking. He crossed to the bed and placed a large hand on the bedpost, leaning his weight upon it. The bed creaked in protest.

"Howdy, Pete," Lazzard said. "How you feeling?"

"I'm okay," Roscoe replied without hesitation. "Get outa here, Martha, and don't listen at the door." He was unshaven, and his face was gaunt. There was a pallor in his cheeks, and his eyes were bright, almost too bright.

Lazzard felt disappointment flood through him. Roscoe looked too ill for this chore. The crook was a good man in his small way, and Lazzard had used him on occasion when he wanted something done that had to be kept secret from his own outfit.

"You're looking bad, Pete. Has the doctor been in to you?"

"Can't afford the Doc," Roscoe replied. "I ain't worked in some time. Got no dough left."

"Can you get outa this bed for a day?" Lazzard demanded.

"How much?"

"Fifty bucks."

"Who'd you want killed?"

Lazzard threw a glance at the door, and lowered his voice.

"Listen, Pete, this is important for me. There's gonna be trouble at the Sutton place tomorrow morning. Whisky Clanton is gonna ride in there with his crew. There should be shooting, but I want to make sure. I want you on hand with your Winchester. There ain't a better shot in the county than you."

"I get it," Roscoe said hoarsely. He pushed himself up off the bed. "Who do you want me to nail; Sutton or Clanton or both of them?"

"You can't shoot both of them," Lazzard said quickly. "Their crews would know it was an outside job then. But if you got Sutton that would really start the gun-smoke drifting."

"What time do you want me out there?" Roscoe demanded.

"Are you well enough to handle it?"

"I'd ride into hell and back right now for fifty bucks."

"Here's the dough." Lazzard produced his wad of notes and counted off the money. Roscoe almost snatched at it, and he counted it. Lazzard watched him with a half smile on his thick lips. "I don't have to tell you how to handle this, Pete, and don't forget that it's mighty important to me that shooting starts on the Broken S when the Circle C shows up there."

"Don't worry about a thing," Roscoe said, grinning. He stuffed the money under his dirty pillow. "I'll get out there by dawn, and when Clanton's outfit shows up I'll put a slug though Sutton. His outfit will think that Clanton staked out a man in ambush. If that doesn't start the battle then I'll do some more shooting."

"But don't cut it fine. I don't want you to get caught, or even seen. Okay?"

"Sure thing. It's as good as done." Roscoe grinned. "When do I see you again?"

"I'll drop by when I need you," Lazzard said. "I'd better get moving now. I don't want to be seen around here. You can trust your woman to keep her trap shut, can you?"

"She knows when she's well off," Roscoe said. "Thanks for dropping by, Ben. I could sure do with this dough."

"There'll be a lot more in the near future if you handle this one right, Pete. I'm starting to clean up, and there are a couple of hombres in the way. I'll pay you a hundred bucks to nail someone mebbe next week."

"Must be a tough guy, you offering a hundred," Roscoe said. "Who is he? If I happen to drop on him on the range I'll take care of him then and there."

"Nope," Lazzard said. "One thing at a time. I know the law ain't much good around here, but I don't want to stir up anything."

"Wickup ain't no great shakes as a lawman," the small-time crook asserted, "and his deputy ain't got much idea. Anyways, they'll have their hands full with the fight that I'll start tomorrow."

"You could be right, Pete." Lazzard stroked his long jaw. His pale eyes glittered in the lamplight. There was a sharp expression on his face as he weighed up the situation. "Yeah, if you do see John Larew's brother around on the range you can put a slug through him."

"John Larew's brother?" Roscoe shook his head. "Didn't know he had one. There ain't no brother out at the Bar Sixty."

"There is now," Lazzard said. "Buck Larew rode in earlier. He's up from Texas, where he's been a Ranger. He's a real tough hombre, Pete. You're gonna have to make sure of him with one shot. If he gets anything like an even break he'll kill you."

"Not me," Roscoe said with a grin. "I ain't never missed with a shot. If I get my sights on him then he's a dead duck."

"Good. You won't be able to mistake him. If you know John Larew then you'll know his brother."

"Tall and dark," Roscoe said, "with brown eyes."

"That's right. He looks a lot like John Larew. You won't mistake when you set eyes on him."

"How about a little on account?" Roscoe demanded. "I'll take a ride around the Bar Sixty tomorrow after I've started your war. Buck Larew will be dead by tomorrow night."

"Here's twenty-five," Lazzard said, peeling the money off his roll. "That's all I can spare until I get into the bank." He grinned to himself when he thought of the raid he planned to make on the morrow. He'd get into the bank all right, and there wouldn't be a lot left by the time he got out again.

"Thanks, Ben. Now don't you worry about a thing. I'll get some sleep now, and I'll be out at the Sutton place by dawn. You'll soon hear how it all went off. Someone will ride in for the law, and he'll sure have a tale to tell."

"Just play it smart, Pete," Lazzard said, moving to the door. He took his leave quickly, and the woman let him out of the cabin. He stood in the shadows for a moment, staring around, then started away back towards the main street. He was whistling under his breath as he gained the sidewalk, and again he stepped into the shadows to peer around. Then he moved forward more boldly, and headed towards the bank. He wanted to take a look around on his own before finalising his plans for the raid. He had to have everything straight in his mind, and although the darkness would hinder his observations, he knew that he couldn't check out the bank during the day.

Lazzard paused in the doorway of the bank, and pushed against the big front door. It was solid and heavy. He wondered if the fact that it would be closed during the raid next day would attract curious attention. Folk in a town such as this were quick to notice anything unusual. He stared around the street. It wouldn't do to have something going wrong so he and Heppell had to run a gauntlet of fire. He moved along the sidewalk to the alley at the side of the building, and was surprised to see a light showing from a side window of the bank. He saw that it was coming from the office of Mart Anders, the bank president.

For a moment Lazzard hesitated. Then he walked quickly along the alley towards the lighted window. He wanted to check out back of the bank, where their horses would be left the next day, and he had to make sure that the area was okay for getting away over.

He reached the window and peered in, and saw the fat figure of Anders seated at a big desk. Sheriff Wickup was seated on a chair at the far corner of the desk, his face towards the window, and Lazzard stared at the two for a moment, straining his ears to pick up what was being said. The window was open a fraction at the top, and the sound of Anders' harsh voice came easily to Lazzard. His eyes glittered when he saw that the door of the massive safe against the back wall of the office was wide open, and there were piles of paper money inside, and leather bags that were bulky with coin and gold. But his pleasure at sight of the money quickly faded as the significance of what was being said inside the office came to him.

"I think your deputy had better travel on the coach in the morning, Bub," Anders said. "As you can see in the safe, there's a lot of money to be shipped, and with the trouble that is building up around here I can't afford to take any chances. I'm a worried man now, having so much dough on the place, but by dawn tomorrow most of it will be gone. I'm keeping just enough on hand to settle the usual business. In future I'm shipping out all extra money as soon as I can."

"Okay, Mart," the sheriff replied, staring with disinterest into the open safe. "I'll have Lee outside here at dawn. He's a good boy. He'll take care of your shipment."

"I'll pay for his services," Anders said. "But I've had a hunch for some time now that we can expect trouble in this town. I've taken precautions though, and any gang that walks in through the front door to try and hold us up will get the shock of their lives."

"Good idea having those shotguns fitted to cover the door," Wickup agreed.

"And they can be fired by anyone at the counter," Anders said. "It's a complicated set-up, but anyone standing at the counter and demanding money will get a bellyful of lead."

Lazzard's blood ran cold as he listened. His eyes widened as he stared in at the two men. So there was a gun trap set for any raiders! He shivered to think how close he had come to setting it off. Shotguns covering the entrance! Hell, that was past a joke. He shook his head. He wasn't walking into this place tomorrow or at any other time to rob it. He needed money to finance his projects, but not so badly that he would risk his life to get it. Then he thought of the situation, and knew that he had to grab some money from somewhere.

The stacks of paper money lying in the big safe looked tempting, and Lazzard lifted a hand to his forehead and wiped away the gathering sweat. He had to get his hands on that dough. And it was being moved out first thing in the morning. He gritted his teeth. That money was right there now, his for the taking. All he had to do was overpower those pair inside and it would be his. But he couldn't walk in there and confront them. They would know him.

Lazzard pressed back into the darkness as the sheriff got to his feet. The lawman was about to leave. Anders got up, pointing to the door.

"I'll let you out the side door, Bub. Like to keep it locked while I'm alone in here."

"I allus reckon you're a mite foolish sitting in here with all that dough in the place."

"This is the bank," Anders reminded.

"Sure, but you should get yourself a night watchman, or someone to keep an eye on the premises," the sheriff went on. "You've got a lot of dough in here."

"I live over the top," the banker said. "I'd hear anything unusual, and I've got a couple of shotguns and some pistols around. I'm a good shot."

They left the office and Lazzard ran quickly along the alley to the back lots. As he stepped into cover behind the corner he heard the door of the building open, and the next moment the sheriff emerged into the alley. Lazzard waited until the lawman had gone into the street. Then he catfooted back to the window, and saw Anders moving back to his desk.

The banker was alone in there with all that money.

The thought hit Lazzard hard. All he had to do was get in there with his gun in his hand and the lot would be his. He licked his lips. This was an opportunity that couldn't be overlooked. If he didn't take it now he wouldn't get the chance to rob the place next day, not with hidden shotguns covering the doorway.

He moved to the side door and tried it, cursing when he found it was locked. But this door was not as heavy as the front entrance. He let his pent up breath go between his stiff lips. How could he get the door open without making a sound?

Then he remembered that the window of the office was open a fraction. He moved back to it and checked. One swift movement would have the window wide, and he could lean in and cover Anders with his Colt. He could climb in and overpower the banker, and the rest would be easy. Lazzard's breathing began to quicken. He moistened his lips. This was a now or never chance! He had to take it or all his plans would fall through for lack of money.

Lifting his gun, Lazzard cocked the heavy weapon. He reached up a long arm and his fingers slid into the crack at the top of the window. He stared balefully at the banker. Anders was working on a list of figures, and suddenly Lazzard heaved on the window. He thinned his lips as it slid down easily. He swung his right hand over the top of the window as he leaped up on to the window sill, and the banker looked up from his work with shock and surprise showing on his suddenly pale features.

Lazzard straightened on the window sill, menacing the banker with his ready gun. He stepped over the window and ducked almost double to get through the aperture. Then he dropped down into the office. He moved quickly towards the desk as the banker reached out a shaking hand to jerk open his right-hand drawer.

"Don't do it, Anders," Lazzard snapped. "I'll kill you if I have to."

"What's the meaning of this, Lazzard?" the banker demanded in quivering tones.

"What the hell do you think?" the rancher snarled. He closed in on the desk while he spoke. His eyes flickered from Anders to the open safe. "I've come to make a withdrawal." He laughed harshly.

"You fool," the banker retorted, overcoming his fears. "How can you hope to get away with it? I'll raise the alarm as soon as you leave."

"Then I'll have to kill you," Lazzard rapped.

"A shot will bring the sheriff running."

"There's more than one way to rope a steer," Lazzard said. He lunged forward suddenly, swiping at the banker's head with the barrel of his pistol. The steel struck heavily just above Anders' ear, and the banker sagged forward with a strangled gasp. Lazzard gritted his teeth and struck again, and blood spurted from Anders' head. Again and again Lazzard struck with the gun barrel, and he cursed fitfully as he pounded the banker to death. The sickening thuds of the furious blows told him that he was cracking the man's skull, and he kept hitting viciously while the blood spurted and spread across the desk.

There was deathly silence when Lazzard finally straightened. He stared down at the limp figure, his eyes hardly taking in the spilled blood. Then he looked anxiously at the uncurtained window. If someone should pass along the alley now he would be in trouble. He moved around the desk and wiped the blood stains from his gun on the banker's coat, and he holstered the weapon and started towards the safe with his mouth dropping open in pleasure at sight of all the money.

A stack of linen bags lay inside the safe, and Lazzard

snatched up a couple and began stuffing them with the stacks of notes. He worked feverishly, and sweat beaded his craggy forehead and trickled down his face. He kept throwing glances at the window, and fear was beginning to move inside him. He didn't spare another glance at the dead banker. He filled the two bags and picked up a third. There was more money here than he had ever seen before, and his hands were trembling as he methodically lifted the piles of notes and stuffed them into empty bags.

He filled five bags in all, and wondered how he was going to carry it all away. He knew that he couldn't walk openly into the hotel, and for a moment the excitement at having got this far with his impulsive robbery almost threw his calculating mind out of gear. He kept glancing around, and impatience was beginning to gnaw at his insides. He wanted to get out of here, but he didn't intend that a single dollar should remain upon the premises.

When he thought he heard a sound outside in the alley he went scurrying to the lamp on the desk and extinguished it. He stood in the darkness, almost leaning over the corpse, and he drew his gun. His senses seemed to be more keener than he could ever recall, and he could hear the dull pounding of his heart. He listened intently, but heard nothing more suspicious, and put it down to his nerves. But he had to fetch help. He couldn't carry this dough away by himself, and he had no intention of doing anything foolish. He moved out of the office, leaving the moneybags where he had placed them. He fumbled through the darkness to the side door, and his groping hands found a key in the lock. He unlocked the door and let himself out into the alley, and locked the door at his back. That would keep everything in order until he could get back. He didn't want any nosey lawman wandering into the office and finding Anders dead. He sighed his relief as he started across the back lots towards the hotel. He would have to rouse out Drago Heppell, and as soon as they had saddled up they would remove the money from the bank. It would be an easy thing to ride out of town and bury the loot, then make it back into Rainbow Creek. They would have to be around in the morning when the robbery and murder were discovered, for Bub Wickup would recall that Lazzard said he intended staying in town overnight.

Some of his excitement fled before the knowledge that he could not afford to make any mistakes now. He took a grip on his fluttering nerves and entered the hotel, glancing down at his clothes to make sure that he was not stained with blood. He approached the desk and asked for his room number, and the clerk did no more than give him a cursory glance before handing over a key. Lazard went up the stairs quickly, and as he unlocked the door of his room Drago Heppell appeared from next door. . . .

CHAPTER 5

BUCK was ready for bed when they sighted the Broken S, but he fought down his tiredness as he put away his horse. A dark figure appeared out of the shadows and challenged them, and Morrell spoke up quickly. The guard came forward, and told them that all was quiet. Buck was thankful for that, but he guessed that Lazzard had made his plans and was sticking to them. The scheming rancher wouldn't stray from his original plot, although he might sidestep some main issue if an opportunity arose that might benefit him by precipitate action.

They crossed the yard to the house and Wire Sutton spoke up from the shadows on the porch.

"What's gone wrong?" the rancher demanded. "I heard your mounts coming in."

"Nothing wrong in that sense," Buck replied. "Let's go into the house and we'll tell you. I reckon it's good news, although it means a fight."

"That sounds ominous," Sutton remarked, stepping into the house and holding open the door. He shut the door after Buck and Morrell had entered, then led the way into his study. "Well?" he demanded. "What's happened?"

"You tell him," Morrell said. "You did all the work. I was just along for the ride."

"Okay." Buck's eyes glinted as he stared at the rancher. He began to speak softly, giving a bare account of what he had overheard at the Lazy L, and what he and Morrell had done about it. By the time he had finished Sutton was on his feet and pacing to and fro like an angry mountain cat. The rancher kept smacking the fist of one hand into the palm of the other.

"So that's how low Lazzard has sunk, huh?" he said suddenly. "Well he's over-stepped the mark this time. Instead of putting Clanton against me with smoking guns he's achieved the opposite. Now we'll have him. I've been waiting a long time for a chance like this."

"No violence until after we've put the law wise to this," Buck warned. "Like I told Clanton. The Lazy L will be a tough bunch to beat. We've got to handle it cleverly."

"I ain't gonna argue with that," Sutton said. "You're getting results, Buck. I wouldn't dream of going against your word now. You're the professional man in all this. You know what to do next."

"That's just the trouble," Buck said slowly. "I don't know. I've arranged for Clanton to show up here with his outfit at dawn, and I figure we should all ride into town to get hold of Ben Lazzard. I heard that he'd gone to Rainbow Creek with his son and a gunman named Drago Heppell. They're staying for a few days. I wonder what's in the wind. Do you think they've left their spread just in case there is trouble between you and Clanton? I mean, he's been angling for this for a long time. Mebbe he won't want to be around when the actual shooting starts."

"It would be like the Lazzards to make for town to get themselves an alibi," Sutton said thickly. "But it won't do them any good this time. We'll get into town tomorrow and lay down the law."

"Yeah, and I'm ready for bed right now," Buck said. "But I got a feeling that something is being planned. Lazzard ain't the kind to run into town and skulk around while an important thing like a war between you and Clanton got under way. I figure that Ben Lazzard would want to be on the spot to take advantage of any situation that might come up."

"So you reckon he's up to no good around town?" Sutton stared at Buck for a moment, his dark eyes filled with enquiry and speculation. "Hell, Buck, you're thinking much too deep for me. But you're used to this kind of thing, worrying out the details and playing hunches. Okay, so you figure that the Lazzards are up to something crooked, and they're gonna use a war between me and Clanton to cover it up for them, is that it?"

"Not exactly what I had in mind, but you might have hit the nail on the head," Buck replied. "I reckon I better ride into Rainbow Creek now."

"Hell," Morrell said, his shoulders sagging. "That means I got to ride with you."

"I can go alone," Buck retorted.

"Like hell," the cowboy said. "I like the way you operate, Buck, and I'll stick with you so long as it's in the interests of the Broken S."

"Sure thing," Sutton said. "You ride along with Buck, Roan, and do everything he tells you. What about the rest of us, Buck? You want for me to wait for Clanton and his boys to show up then head into town behind you?"

"Yeah," Buck said. He nodded slowly, his mind working on the details. "Like I said before, we can take the two Lazzards and the gunman with them before the rest of their outfit know what's happening. That'll prevent a lot of shooting and bloodshed. Me and Morrell will ride out now, if we can have a couple of fresh horses, and we'll snoop around town and find out what Ben Lazzard has been up to around here. It might be vital to our plan."

Morrell made for the door. He grinned wearily at Buck.

"I'll get a couple of mounts saddled up," he said. "Come on out in a couple of minutes."

Buck nodded. He sat down again and relaxed. What the hell was he doing chasing around all hours God made? He thought he'd left all that behind him in Texas with the Ranger badge he'd turned in. But this was a job that had to be done if he wanted to settle down on the Bar Sixty with his brother and raise cows.

"I wish you luck," Sutton said when Buck sighed and got to his feet. "I feel a lot easier now than I've done for some time. There was a real bad situation building up around here."

"But a few sensible words have sorted out most of it," Buck retorted. "Men are fools, Sutton. They start squaring up to each other before they think. If one of you around here had his wits about him he would have seen that someone was stirring up the trouble for the others. You should have spotted that."

"I guess so. I knew Lazzard was behind most of my trouble, but instead of figuring that he was causing it between me and Clanton I reckoned that Clanton was stepping in to grab himself something."

"Well you ain't got anything else to fight Clanton over," Buck said, starting for the door. "That water-hole won't be fit for use for a good many years, if ever again."

"You're right. Mind your step in Rainbow Creek. That Drago Heppell is a real tough hombre, and mighty fast with a gun. Play it cool until we show up. Then we can throw our weight about for a bit."

Buck went out into the night and crossed to the corral. Morrell was waiting for him, already in the saddle on a fresh mount, and Buck suppressed a sigh as he mounted another horse and took up the reins.

"If you're ready," he said to Morrell. "We're getting

our share of riding, but one thing stands out. This chore should be over and done with by tomorrow."

"If it pans out right," the cowboy said, showing his teeth in a brief smile. "There's many a slip, you know."

"Yeah, and that's what I'm afraid of," Buck admitted. "I've been in this kind of a situation more times than I care to remember, and many's the time I thought I had a case under control. But you never can tell. Some of these scheming men are really clever, and they take some beating."

They rode out and Morrell started the long ride to Rainbow Creek. Buck was not inclined to conversation now, and he half-dozed in his saddle, a trick he had learned while working for the Rangers. When a man had countless miles to travel he did what he could for himself in the way of sleep and rest. If he could then he unrolled his blankets for a couple of hours at a time, and a man could maintain himself for long periods with only occasional brief snatches of sleep. But if time was too urgent then he had to do the best he could, and the answer was to doze in the saddle, taking it in turns with a pard.

Morrell set a fast pace, and the miles dropped behind. There was no moon, but the starlight was good enough to permit them long vision. Their eyes were accustomed to the darkness, and they watched their surroundings, for this county was plagued with trouble and unrest.

They hit the main trail that led into town, and Buck straightened in his saddle. Their hoofs pounded loudly on the hard ground. It was long past midnight and the range was asleep. Morrell slowed, then halted to give their mounts a rest, and they both stepped from their saddles and dropped their reins. Morrell rolled a smoke and lit it, and Buck refused the offer of the makings. He walked off a couple of yards and stared around into the shadows. He felt stark and cold, lonely despite Morrell's presence. Thought of most of the men in the county now at rest made him shake his head. He was a Johnny-come-lately, but already he was caught up in this business.

He stiffened as the sound of hoofbeats came to his ears, and he moved back to Morrell's side, who had already extinguished his cigarette.

"Two riders coming," the cowboy announced. "They're moving fast for this time of night."

"Coming from the direction of the town," Buck added. "We better play this smart just in case they aren't friendly. We don't know what the Lazzards might have been up to in Rainbow Creek."

Morrell was already moving to his mount, and he tightened the cinch and held his mount's nose to prevent any sound. Buck quickly did the same, and moments later two horsemen appeared briefly out of the night as they went past on the trail. Morrell bent a little at the knees to get the two in silhouette, and after they had gone by he turned to Buck.

"One of them was Ben Lazzard," he said.

"That certain?" Buck demanded.

"I know the skunk well," the cowboy retorted. "Now what do you suppose has made him go riding fast through the night? Ben Lazzard is known for his laziness. He won't do a damn thing that requires energy. He ain't a working rancher, if you get my meaning."

"Then I reckon we better follow him and see what he is up to," Buck retorted.

"Don't know about that." Morrell stared into the night in the direction taken by the two riders. "It'll be difficult following them without giving ourselves away. They're travelling too fast for us to get close enough to see them without the sound of our hoofs warning them of our presence. I reckon we better sift into town and find out what's been happening. Mebbe they started something there which is meant to tie in with the battle that's supposed to take place out at our spread in the morning."

"You're going deep with your reasoning," Buck said with a grin, "and I reckon you'd make a good lawman with some practice, Morrell."

"I'm happy enough in my own job," the cowboy replied. "From what I know about it, a lawman's life is all ride and sweat. It wouldn't be so bad if his work was done during the day, but it's mostly night work, huh?"

"That's because most of the badmen are moving around at night when honest folk are in bed." Buck shook his head at recollection of some of his experiences. "Come on, let's hit that town."

They mounted and continued, and now there was no sleepiness in them. They were wondering if something had happened in town. Ben Lazzard was playing a deep game that was controlled by complicated rules, and until the whole plan was bared the bones of it would remain a mystery to anyone trying to figure out what was going on. Buck let his trained mind sort through the leaping details that were fed through his brain. One thing was certain, he decided. This business was pushing for a showdown, and he had arrived in time to catch it. But he was glad that he had showed up. His brother seemed to be in the thick of it, and if the shooting had started before Buck arrived then he might have come on the scene in time to bury John.

Morrell pushed on fast, and the cowboy didn't spare his horse. Buck kept beside the man, and they didn't waste breath on talk. The miles slipped by, and then they spotted tiny lights glimmering in the distance. Morrell reined up to rest the horses.

"They allus leave a few lanterns burning along the

street," the cowboy said. "Makes it easier for the patrol-
ling lawman to keep an eye on things."

"The West is becoming civilised," Buck replied with
a faint grin. "It'll be the day when men won't have to
pack guns with them everywhere they go."

"That'll be the great step towards civilisation,"
Morrell agreed.

They went on, and rode into the outskirts of the town.
Morrell headed for the stable, and the sound of their
hoofs echoed around the quiet street. They dismounted
and watered their horses at the trough, then led them
into the lofty barn and put them in stalls. They unsaddled
and bedded down the animals, then left the stable and
walked slowly along the sidewalk, making for the hotel.

"Will we be able to get room this time of the night?"
Buck demanded.

"Yeah. They have a night-clerk," Morrell said. "We'll
get in. But we ain't gonna get much shut-eye. Dawn
ain't far away."

"We ain't got to get up too early," Buck retorted. "If
things are doing out at the Broken S at dawn it ain't
none of our business, and our reinforcements won't get
into town before mid-morning."

"Okay, so we'll get some rest." Morrell paused for a
moment and stared at Buck. "But I figure we oughta
find out if anything has happened around here lately."

"Sheriff's office?" Buck asked.

"Could try. There'll be a lawman on duty. But do
we mention that we saw Lazzard haring along the trail
out of town?"

"I don't think so." Buck thought about it for a
moment. "We want to keep this as quiet as possible until
we know what's going on. Mebbe we better forget everything until morning. It's gonna sound mighty suspicious
to a lawman if we walk in on him and ask if there's been

any trouble around town. And if there has then he's gonna wonder if we had anything to do with it."

"You're right." Morrell started forward again and Buck walked beside the cowboy. "Come on, let's get some sleep and be up and ready for anything when the sun shows."

They went to the hotel, and found a lamp burning low in the entrance. There was an old man asleep in a chair behind the reception desk, and Morrell grinned as he reached across and touched the oldster's shoulder. The clerk came awake with a snort, and blinked at them for a moment before moving. Then he stifled a yawn and stretched.

"Want a room?" he demanded.

"Just for tonight," Buck said.

"For half a night," Morrell corrected. "Do we get one half price, Zeke?"

"Nope." There was no humour in the oldster at this time of night.

"Got many rooms occupied?" Buck demanded.

"Business is good." The old man jerked a thumb at the dog-eared register. "Sign your names in there. You can have Room Eleven. It's up on the first floor."

"I see you've got Ben Lazzard in tonight," Buck observed, his alert eyes scanning the previous signatures as he signed his name.

"Yeah, and him and most of the other guests were in bed early, so don't make any noise when you go up," the clerk warned. "I know what you cowboys are."

Morrell took the key and they went up the stairs to the first floor. On the landing Buck paused and glanced around. He saw the room that Lazzard had taken, and motioned to Morrell.

"See if that key fits Lazzard's door," he said. "We better make sure it was Lazzard you saw on the trail."

"What if he is inside?" Morrell demanded. "He might start shooting if we bust in on him."

"We can always pretend we got the wrong room," Buck retorted.

"This key will open every door in the building," the cowboy said, moving to the door. "All the locks are the same pattern."

He trust the key into the lock and turned it easily. The door opened quietly, and Buck craned forward. There was enough light from the low-burning lamp in the passage to permit him to see inside the room, and the bed was empty.

"Drago Heppell, Lazzard's pet gunman, has the room next door," Morrell said. "Let's take a look and find out if he was the hombre on the trail with Lazzard." He locked the door of Lazzard's room and went on to the next. The key again unlocked the door, and they peered inside. The room was empty.

"That clinches it," Buck said as they went on to their room. "It was Lazzard you saw."

They entered their room, and saw two single beds. Morrell lit a lamp, and then put the key into the lock and turned it. He crossed to the nearer bed and sat down upon it with a heavy sigh bursting from him. He removed his gunbelt and boots and dropped back on the bed, lifting his feet from the floor and slumping relaxed. He closed his eyes, then opened them and stared at Buck, who was taking off his boots.

"I wonder why Lazzard took a room for the night, then decided to ride out at this early hour?" he demanded.

"I'll ask him in the morning," Buck said, grinning tiredly. "We ain't gonna find out the answer until then, so forget about it. The whole town is pretty quiet, so nothing serious could have happened."

"Mebbe you're right." Morrell closed his eyes again and relaxed. He fell asleep almost instantly.

Buck got into the bed. He reached out a long arm and turned out the lamp. When darkness swooped in upon him he closed his eyes and let go his hold upon his determination. Weariness speared through him. His legs were throbbing with exhaustion. His mind fluttered with thought, but he relaxed and smoothed out his worries. He drifted into sleep, but part of his brain seemed to remain alert. He didn't sleep well. There was too much on his mind. He kept rising from the depths, coming half awake to stare around the unfamiliar room, and although he didn't fully awake he noted that dawn was breaking. Some time later he half sat up when he heard a noise in the passage outside, and then the door of the next room opened gently. The door squeaked on its hinges as it closed. That was Drago Heppell's room, Buck thought. So Lazzard and his gunman had returned. He forgot about the situation then and went back to sleep, and he lay unmoving until Roan Morrell shook him awake. . . .

The sun was flooding into the room when Morrell's voice broke into Buck's mind, and he started and opened his eyes. He glanced at the cowboy, who was rubbing his eyes. Then he looked around the room.

"I feel as if I ain't closed my eyes at all," Morrell said. "The hell with riding through half the night. I could sleep right through until tomorrow morning."

"Me too," Buck commented, getting out of the bed. He began to dress. "But this is an important day for us. By the way, I heard Heppell's door open and shut just before dawn. I'm wondering if Lazzard came back with him."

"Mebbe it wasn't Heppell we saw with Ben Lazzard," Morrell said.

"Of course." Buck looked up from cleaning his gun. His brown eyes glittered. "Ike Lazzard rode into town with those two yesterday. Mebbe it was him with his father."

"Yeah, that's what I'm figuring," Morrell said. "Heppell could have been busy around town. There's no telling what kind of hell he was raising on Lazzard's orders."

"While Lazzard himself was heading back to his ranch, huh?" Buck shook his head as he considered it. He reckoned Lazzard was more than ordinarily smart. It was going to take a lot to pin anything on the scheming rancher, even if proof of what had happened at Clanton's waterhole could be pinned on the Lazy L outfit. Lazzard would see to it that his men took the rap for him. He would have engaged them on that basis, and no doubt the gunmen would remain loyal to him.

"Let's go get some grub," Morrell said, buckling his gun around his waist. He moved to the door and unlocked it. Buck followed him out.

They went down to the dining room and took a corner table. Morrell glanced around, and then stiffened. The cowboy cursed half under his breath, and Buck glanced at his companion.

"Over there at the window," Morrell said. "It's Ben Lazzard and Heppell."

"Yeah," Buck said thinly, staring across the wide room. "So Lazzard came back when Heppell did. They couldn't have got all the way back to the Lazy L, then returned here in the time, could they?"

"Nope. They certainly didn't go back to their ranch," Morrell confirmed. "It was about half-two when we saw them. They'd be a long way from here if they did make it to the Lazy L after they passed us."

"They couldn't have got to the Broken S or my

brother's place and back in the time either." Buck
frowned. What lay behind it? "Whatever they did, they
wanted it to appear that they've been in their rooms all
night. Order some breakfast, Roan, then we'll mosey
along to the stable and take a look at their hosses. If
they've been hard ridden for a long way it'll show in
the animals."

Morrell nodded and called to a hovering waitress. He
ordered breakfast, and they didn't have long to wait
before the meal arrived. They both fell to with enthu-
siasm, and as they ate Buck wondered about the meeting
between Clanton and Sutton. The two ranchers would
be suspicious of each other still, but a few words together
would soon straighten them both out, and as they now
knew that they had been duped by Ben Lazzard they
would unite to fight the threat against their security.

Buck had just pushed aside his plate and picked up
his coffee when a man came running into the dining hall.
He halted on the threshhold and stared around, looking
for no one in particular. There was a tense expression on
his face, and he didn't remain still for longer than a split
second before he started out the door, but he yelled out
excitedly at the top of his voice.

"Anders at the bank has been found dead with his
head bashed in, and the big safe is empty."

Morrell started to his feet immediately, spilling his
coffee in his haste. Buck set down his cup, his eyes flit-
ting immediately to Ben Lazzard, and the rancher
happened to be glancing in his direction at the same
time. But there was no expression on the rancher's smooth
features. The other occupants of the room were already
rushing for the door, and Lazzard got up, followed by
Heppell, and came towards the door.

Buck turned and hurried after Morrell, and caught up
with the cowboy out on the sidewalk. Word of what had

happened at the bank had quickly got around the town, and the wide street was thronged with hurrying people all making for the bank. There were something like a hundred men and women crowding in front of the building, and more were arriving at every minute.

Morrell pushed his way to the front of the crowd and found a deputy standing on the sidewalk in front of the bank. The big door was closed. The noise of many excited voices yelling for details of the murder and robbery was almost deafening. Buck thinned his lips. He had seen this sort of thing many times before, and he glanced around at the hoarsely calling men. The sheriff would have his hands filled with trying to control this bunch. Perhaps he could do with some help.

Buck stepped on to the sidewalk and approached the deputy, whose youthful face was wearing deep shock. He was a tall, lean youngster in his early twenties, and he stared intently at Buck, who had to shout to make himself heard above the voices.

"I'm Buck Larew, an ex-Texas Ranger. Mebbe I can be of some help. Where's the sheriff?"

"He's inside," the deputy said thickly. "You can go on in and see him if you want."

"Thanks." Buck moved to the heavy door and turned the handle. He stepped into the bank and swung the door shut at his back. A couple of townsmen stood just inside the bank, and they looked enquiringly at Buck. "Where's the sheriff?" he asked them.

"Down at the far end. First door on the right," he was told.

He went along the counter, his boots thudding loudly, and he entered the narrow passage and knocked on the first door on the right. It was jerked open immediately, and the sheriff stood before him, shock written plainly on his leathery cheeks.

"Who are you?" Wickup demanded.

"Buck Larew, John Larew's brother. I've been a lawman in my time, and I figured you could do with some professional help around here. You've sure got a big crowd out there yelling around."

"Sure," Wickup said slowly. "Glad to know you, Larew. Come on in."

Buck entered the office and glanced at the man bending over the still figure slumped on the desk. He saw plenty of spilled blood around.

"That's Doc Williams," the sheriff said, and the medico looked up from his grim task and nodded at Buck, who lifted a hand. "John Larew's brother Buck, Seth."

"Head battered in," Buck said. "Have you got a line on the killer?"

"Hell, he wasn't found until Lee, my deputy, came here to report for duty," Wickup said in shaking tones. "There was a big money shipment due out this morning on the coach. Someone sure laid his plans close. I was in here last evening talking to Anders. He was saying how he figured that someone might take a crack at his dough. Damn me if they haven't! I don't know where to start first."

"How did the robbers get in?" Buck asked.

"Through that window." Wickup pointed to the opened window in the office. "Lee Paine came here earlier and found the bank locked. He hung around, and then figured that Anders had overslept. He went down the side alley that side and called up to Anders' apartment, but got no reply. He walked around the back of the building and entered the other alley this side, and saw the open window. When he looked in he saw Anders sprawled there, with blood all over the place."

"Was that window open last night when you were here?" Buck demanded.

"Hell, I don't know. I never noticed." The sheriff shook his head. "What the hell am I gonna do?"

"What happened when you left, and what time would that be?" Buck pursued.

"I dunno really. I was making my rounds. It was getting on in the evening. Couldn't have been before nine, and likely was after ten. I stayed some time talking, and then Anders let me out the side door. He locked it afterwards. I heard the key turn in the lock before I moved away. I'd only been telling him to get a night-watchman in to keep an eye on things, but he wouldn't hear of it."

"So the robbery took place between the time you left and the deputy saw the body." Buck moved closer to the desk and stared at the bloodstains. They were dry in places, only the bigger stains looking wet at their gory centres. He looked at the doctor as the medico straightened. "Can you give us some idea what time he was killed, Doc?" he asked.

"Can't say for certain. It was a real cold night last night. But I reckon it happened between half-past ten last night and midnight. That's as near as I can put it. He was battered to death with a blunt instrument. I guess you can see that for yourself."

The sheriff came up beside Buck and stared at the corpse.

"If only he could talk," he said helplessly.

"Mebbe he can, indirectly," Buck said. "Have you had a good look around? The killer might have left a clue of some sort."

"I didn't touch anything," the sheriff told him. "I wanted the Doc to get through first."

"Well I've done all I can," the doctor said. "I'm sorry I couldn't be more helpful."

The medico gathered up his bag and departed. Buck

moved around the desk and stared at the corpse, glancing around to get the distances of the office in his mind. The sheriff watched him silently, his face showing that he was out of his depth in this.

"The robber, or robbers, came in through the window, huh?" Buck demanded. "The banker didn't get to his feet, unless they made him sit down again." He lapsed into silence when he realized that he wasn't making any headway. He stared on the floor, looking for anything that might have been left by the killer. There was nothing. He crossed to the safe and looked inside. It was empty of money. "How much was in there?" he asked. "You got any idea?"

"Not exactly," Wickup said. "But I looked in it last night. The door stood open, and that top shelf was filled with piles of notes. There were some leather bags of coin and gold on the next shelf. It's all gone. The place has been cleaned out."

"How many men in town?" Buck demanded.

"About a hundred, I'd say. Why?"

"Because you're gonna have to question every last one of them about their movements last night," Buck said crisply. "Someone might have noticed something suspicious. A bunch of men might have been seen around here, or the horses that were used to cart away the money. It's a certainty that the robber couldn't carry it himself."

"You're right," Wickup said. "Say, you're pretty smart, Larew. I've been on the look-out for an additional deputy. Would you be interested in the job?"

"Yes," Buck said without hesitation. His mind was working fast. With the situation moving quickly towards some kind of a climax he would be in a good position to handle any real trouble if he was wearing a law badge. "I'll work with you until this present trouble is settled."

"I'll take you on a temporary basis," the sheriff said.

"Let me swear you in now. I've got a deputy badge in my pocket right here. I'm gonna need all the help I can get."

Buck nodded. He lifted his right hand and the sheriff swore him into office. He took the deputy badge with his eyes narrowed, and he pinned it to his shirt front. Now he was a member of the local law department he could do much to cure its apathy. He would soon get to the roots of the trouble. . . .

CHAPTER 6

PETE ROSCOE was at the Broken S ranch before the sun came up. He had a hard ride of it through the night, and reeled out of his saddle when he reached the spot he had been making for. He staggered as he led his horse into cover some two hundred yards south of the ranch house. There was a raging pain in his abdomen, and he felt ill. His hands were shaky and his senses erratic. He had a fever, and spots danced before his eyes. He drew his Winchester from the saddleboot and made his way through thick brush and rocks to a point where he would be able to observe the whole of the ranch. The dawn was breaking as he hunkered down. He cocked his rifle and laid it down, and rested his forehead upon his arms, closing his eyes, shivering in the cold breeze. He felt ill, and had begun to wish that he hadn't taken up Ben Lazzard's offer. But the money would come in handy. He needed that.

The sun came up over the eastern horizon, and Pete lifted his head and peered around. The ground in the middle-distance seemed to be undulating like a green sea, and he kept snapping his eyes to get them clear of the condition, but he was ill, and he knew it. There was a bitter taste in his mouth as he checked his rifle. He would soon have some work to do, and then a fast ride out of it. He recalled Lazzard's words that he was not to be seen by anyone. He wished that he felt better. He peered around.

For some time he was content to rest. He should never have got out of bed. He thinned his lips and forced

determination into his mind. Now he had some money
he could hunt up the Doc after this and get some attention. He had been feeling low for a long time, and
recently he had worsened a little each day. He cursed
under his breath as a twinge of pain seemed to send fire
through his belly. What the hell was wrong with him?

He heard hoofs in the distance and stiffened. He
looked around, and soon spotted a lone rider coming
towards the ranch. He blinked his eyes, and his normally excellent sight soon gave him details of the horse-
man. It was John Larew. But where was the ex-Ranger,
Buck Larew? He could finish off both chores at the same
time if Buck Larew showed up.

Roscoe gazed around expectantly, but failed to spot
anyone else. He shook his head and gazed back at the
ranch. There were a couple of men moving around the
yard, and smoke was beginning to wisp up from the
cookshack stovepipe. He took up his rifle, gazing in the
direction he expected Clanton and the rest of the Circle C
outfit to show from. He would take Clanton with his
first shot. That should start the Circle C shooting at the
Broken S, and if it didn't then he'd do some fast shooting
at Sutton's outfit. In a situation like this it only needed
one shot to start a war. He grinned as he thought about
it. He would be directly responsible for it all.

Minutes passed, and he dropped his head to his arms
again. He was feeling weak and shivery. His mouth was
hot and dry, and the pains in his abdomen were gradually
spreading through his body. He felt worse than he had
done yesterday, and that had been bad enough. He
opened his eyes again and saw John Larew moving into
the Broken S yard. A couple of figures were standing on
the porch now, and he recognised one as Wire Sutton.

The rancher would be his second target, he decided,
and looked again for sign of Clanton and his outfit. He

knew that he would have to move fast after his action, in case any of the men below saw his gunsmoke. He didn't feel up to a long chase, and if he was spotted they wouldn't relinquish pursuit until they'd got him.

Then he heard hoofbeats in the distance, and soon spotted a dust cloud coming forward from the direction of the Clanton place. He gritted his teeth, trying to draw upon his reserves of strength, but his illness had sapped him, and he trembled as he prepared to start a range war.

Riders soon materialised out of the dust, and Roscoe counted seven men. He lifted his rifle, glancing into the Broken S yard. The Sutton crew were gathering by the corral, and Sutton himself was standing on the porch with John Larew. Roscoe settled himself and looked for Whisky Clanton among the oncoming horsemen.

He spotted the big rancher at the head of his men, and began to estimate the range. He checked the strength of the wind, and the speed of the riders, but Clanton was slowing cautiously as he approached the yard. There had been bad blood between the two ranchers for a long time, and it couldn't be wiped away in a single moment. Sutton was stepping off the porch, moving out into the open to greet Clanton, and the watching Roscoe noted that horses were ready saddled by the corral. Things were about to start. Some of the Broken S hands were already climbing into their saddles.

Roscoe lifted his rifle and squinted through the sights, lining up the barrel, and the muzzle gaped at a spot just above the ears of Clanton's mount. The rancher was coming into the yard at a walk, and Roscoe nodded to himself. This was an easy shot. He restrained his breathing and concentrated upon the shot. His illness was forgotten. His weakness seemed to drain away. He paused for a fraction of a second, then gently, almost lovingly, squeezed his trigger.

The Winchester bucked in his expert hands, and the flat crack of the shot hammered through the still air, echoing away time and again. Down in the yard Clanton clutched at his chest and went sideways out of his saddle, and dust flew as his heavy body hit the yard. Everyone else down there was transfixed for the moment, and Roscoe reloaded quickly and shifted his aim. He fired at Sutton, and again the sound of the shot seemed to race across the country. Wire Sutton threw wide his arms and twisted sharply. He went sprawling forward to the ground, pushing his face into the dust.

Then the shock that held the rest of them still was broken. Cowboys started running for cover, drawing their Colts as they moved. Roscoe continued shooting, and he saw a Broken S man twist and fall, to lie still. Then he turned his attention to the mounted Circle C cowboys, and three fast, accurate shots smashed into their close ranks. Two of them slid out of their saddles as the echoes died away.

The rest of the riders were pulling their guns, and shooting broke out rapidly. The Circle C men began to toss lead at the running Broken S punchers, and when they turned to reply, Roscoe grinned happily. That was it. He lay listening to the shooting, watching the movements below, and now he held his fire. He didn't want to give away his position. In the shock of the ambush none of those men down there had seen his smoke. He had accomplished what he came for. Now he had to get away unseen.

He began to push himself back from his position. The pains inside him were worse than before. He groaned in his agony. Sickness seemed to well up inside. He took a deep breath, and the gunsmoke didn't help him any. It was heavy and acrid, choking in his nostrils. He took one last look at the yard below, and was pleased to see the fight that was raging. Clanton still lay where he had fallen, but Sutton was slithering back towards the house. Roscoe looked for John Larew, and frowned when he didn't see the Bar Sixty rancher. He checked the windows of the house for gunsmoke, wondering if Larew had ducked into the building for cover, and then he saw that Larew's horse was gone from the front of the house.

Roscoe paused. He didn't want any pursuit now. He didn't feel up to running for it. He would have a tough time of it now, trying to get into Rainbow Creek to the Doc's place. He cocked his rifle. If John Larew had spotted him up here then the rancher would soon be showing from around the back of the house. That would give him a clear shot. He rested on his elbows, rifle at the ready, eyes narrowed and watching for movement. The sounds of the heavy shooting below rolled over his head in a continuous wave. He saw more still figures in the yard, and grinned happily. Ben Lazzard would be pleased with this.

A rider suddenly appeared from the back of the house, making for Roscoe's position at a gallop. The ambusher lifted his Winchester. He grinned tightly as he took aim. The blob of his foresight covered the head of the approaching horse, and Roscoe waited it out until the animal drew even nearer. Then he lifted his aim a fraction, allowed for the breeze, and fired.

The crack of the rifle was hurled away, and mingled with the heavier sounds of the shooting taking place at the ranch. Roscoe saw the approaching horse fall to its knees, and Larew kicked his feet out of his stirrups as he was sent flying over the animal's head. The horse cartwheeled, and then lay with threshing legs. Roscoe reloaded quickly, ready to toss a slug into John Larew, but the rancher had been hurled out of sight, and he did not re-appear.

Roscoe waited, teeth clenched, and he kept wincing at the surging pains inside him. What the hell was wrong? he wondered. He took a deep breath, but that didn't help, and he began to slither back from his position. He had to get astride his horse and move out of here now before anyone discovered where those first shots had come from. He looked once more at the yard, and the shooting was going on with undiminished fury. There was still no sign of John Larew. He looked for the rancher, but failed to spot movement in the area where Larew had gone to ground. Perhaps his bullet had taken the horse through the head, then hit Larew, he thought. He began to edge away.

When he was out of sight of the ranch he pushed himself up to his hands and knees, holding his rifle in his right hand, and began to crawl towards his horse. The pain in his belly was like a loose rock inside, and he gritted his teeth. Sweat came to his forehead. He was a sick man, and he shouldn't be out here like this. But he had earned his pay, and when he got better he'd see about killing Buck Larew. Then he would collect the rest of his dough from Ben Lazzard.

A bullet clipped his hatbrim, and Roscoe moved so fast in his shock and surprise that for a moment he forgot his pains and illness. He dropped flat, his instincts telling him the direction from which danger threatened, and he rolled over to face the danger, lifting his rifle quickly. He spotted movement to the left and started shooting. He was an expert gunman, better with a Winchester than a Colt, and he sent his lead into the exact spot he wanted to hit. Gunsmoke blew away from him, and he slitted his eyes and peered around. Must be John Larew, he thought.

Nothing moved for several moments, and he began to think that he had nailed the rancher. But he couldn't afford to take chances. He was not agile enough to handle this in his usual manner. He would have to play a waiting game, and hope that none of the men fighting in the yard below would come to investigate.

He moved slightly, rolling slowly into a hollow, and he tried to get comfortable. There was burning fire in his belly, and anger began to well up inside him. Everything seemed to happen to him. But he had no regrets. He had always played his game as he saw it. He took pay for killing, and he delivered the goods; a chunk of lead through somebody's heart. He strained his ears for stealthy sounds. Perhaps Larew was creeping up on him. But he couldn't hear anything except the hammering guns in the yard.

Roscoe felt sick. He hung his head and closed his eyes. He didn't care for the moment if he was caught or not. He began to feel afraid. There must be something seriously wrong with him, and he'd been a fool to delay a visit to the doctor. Now he had to get to town as soon as he could. The doctor could help him.

He eased forward and peered around. No sign of anyone. He eased out of the hollow and started crawling through the brush. It was hard work, and sweat stood out on his face. He hurt his elbows and knees on the rough ground, and began to long for his bed. He'd been a crazy fool to attempt this, he told himself. But he had needed the money desperately, and now he was in a spot. He would have to get clear, and his rifle could manage that for him. He paused time and again to look around, but he didn't see sign of anyone.

Roscoe's horse was stamping in the distance, and he nodded to himself, taking heart from the noise. Once he got into his saddle he'd get away. His only hope was that he would be able to remain in his saddle until he got back to Rainbow Creek. Thought of the many miles that lay between him and rest almost finished him then and there. But he shrugged aside the surging weakness. He had to get out of here.

He sighted his horse, and was moving very slowly. Then he saw something else. A figure was moving stealthily through the brush on the far side of the animal. Roscoe thinned his lips. Someone was getting into an ambush position against him! He thought he recognised John Larew, and cursed silently. It was proof that he was ill! If he'd been his old self he wouldn't have had to throw more than one slug at Larew. He took a long breath, and almost choked as pain stabbed him deeply and made him wince. He lifted his rifle and fired in a swift movement, hardly seeming to aim, and John Larew twisted awkwardly and fell into the brush.

That should teach him! Roscoe thought grimly. He pushed himself forward, wanting to drop flat and rest, but knowing that he had to keep going. There would be plenty of time for rest later. He crawled towards his horse, eyes slitted, watching for movement that would warn him of Larew's activities. He held his rifle as steady as he could, and then started to his feet. His legs almost refused to hold him, and he fell forward on to his knees, cursing his weakness. He could still hear the sound of shooting in the background, and that pleased him. He got up again and staggered towards his horse, keeping the animal between him and the spot where Larew had disappeared. He reached the animal and lifted his left foot to the stirrup. It took all his strength to mount, and he peered around quickly as he gained the saddle. His eyes were glittering, slitted and alert. He was breathing fast, shallowly, and the pain in his belly seemed to be rising all the time, growing in intensity.

Roscoe kept hold of the rifle as he wheeled the horse away from the ranch. He would have to make a slight detour to get away unseen, but that didn't matter now. He was astride a horse, and so long as he remained in the saddle he could keep moving.

As he whirled by the spot where Larew had vanished he glanced down and saw the rancher stretched out on his back. There was a spreading stain of blood on Larew's shirtfront, and Roscoe was tempted to halt and put another slug through the rancher to make sure of him, but he was hanging on to his mount. If he relaxed his grip he would fall to the ground, and somehow he knew that if he got down again he would never regain his seat. He galloped away, cursing the pain that was like a jagged knife inside him. The violent motions of the fast moving horse didn't help him any, but as he drew clear he began to breathe a lot easier. He had made it. Now he could get out of it and collect what Ben Lazzard owed him.

He twisted once in his saddle and cursed when he saw John Larew rising up off the ground. The rancher lifted his Colt and began to empty the weapon in Roscoe's direction, and the gunman turned to face his front and hunched himself in the saddle. The horse galloped on, and several times Roscoe thought he was parting company with the animal. His rifle slipped out of his grasp and hit the ground. Roscoe cursed fitfully, but he did not attempt to stop. He could always get himself another weapon. He rode fast and went over a crest. The next instant there was ground rearing up between him and trouble, and he continued fast without looking around. When he finally drew clear of the vicinity he slowed his horse and allowed the animal to travel at a moderate pace. He lolled in his saddle, almost out of his head now he had no longer to concentrate upon his grim job. He headed back to town. . . .

John Larew cursed angrily when his hammer clicked on an empty chamber, and he dropped back to the ground and sat watching Roscoe make his getaway. There was pain inside his chest, where one of Roscoe's slugs had caught him a glancing blow, but it was nothing like the agony in his mind. He had seen Sutton fall as if dead, and Whisky Clanton, and he could still hear the sounds of shooting going on at the ranch. He hadn't recognised Pete Roscoe, but he'd got a good look at the gunman's horse, and he'd know that again if he saw it. He reloaded his gun with trembling fingers and pushed himself to his feet. He stared around for a moment then started wearily back to the ranch. He had to stop the shooting somehow. He had to get it to those men down there that they had been duped into shooting at each other.

He staggered over the rough ground, his thoughts bitter. He had hardly believed his ears when Sutton told him about Buck's trip to the Lazy L and subsequent visit to Clanton. He knew of the bad blood that existed between the Broken S and the Circle C, and this seemed almost too good to be true; that Buck had got proof against Ben Lazzard, and the Broken S and the Circle C were uniting against the Lazy L. When Clanton and his outfit had ridden into the yard there had been no thought in his mind that trouble might break out. Clanton had been smiling as he came forward to greet them, and then the bullet had struck the Circle C rancher.

Larew alone had spotted the position of the ambusher. At first, in that split second of inactivity, when shock held them all silent and still while Clanton tumbled from his saddle, Larew had caught the sound of the ambusher's muzzle report, and he had stared in that direction while his mind tried to explain the incident. Then the two outfits had started shooting at each other, and Larew caught a glimpse of Roscoe and ducked the fight to get after the man who started it. But all he had done was collect a wound himself, and he gritted his teeth as he came in sight of the ranch.

He halted and stared down at the drifting gunsmoke. It was a grim sight, and he shook his head hopelessly as he lurched forward and made down the slope to the yard. His brother had appeared on the spot only the day before, and in a few short hours had taken control of the situation and started the whole mess of troubles towards a solution. Now complication had reared up, and this was worse now than it had ever been.

Larew wondered about the man who had ridden away. He had not recognised him, and scratched around in his mind for recognition of the fleeing figure. It hadn't been one of Ben Lazzard's outfit, he was sure of that. So who else would have profited from this open war between the two ranchers?

He started down the slope, his gun in its holster, and he set his teeth grimly as he neared the yard. He was closest to the surviving Circle C outfit, and moved in cautiously. He could see some of Clanton's cowboys stretched out lifeless, and Clanton himself was still lying in the dust.

A cowboy swung around to face Larew, and lifted his gun. Larew was holding his hands away from his waist, and he shouted for the man to hold his fire. Other Circle C men turned around, and guns covered Larew. But he was recognised, and he closed in, holding a hand to his chest, covering the patch of blood that marked the strike of Roscoe's shot.

"Hold your fire for God's sake," Larew said grimly,

dropping to cover as lead from the Broken S crew came screeching past him.

"What the hell for?" one of the cowboys demanded. "There's our boss stretched out dead in the yard. The Broken S started that. They lured us into an ambush, and your brother helped to set it up. He rode into our place last night and said that Lazzard's crew had poisoned the waterhole. We fell for it, but it's obvious now that Sutton arranged all that. He's always been after that water, and because he couldn't get it he poisoned it."

"You're talking through your hat," John Larew snapped. "Listen to me. I was standing on the porch when you rode in. I'd just arrived myself. I saw Clanton shot out of his saddle, and I saw something else; the smoke from the rifle that fired the shot. It came from the top of that slope up there." He turned and pointed. "I ducked around the house when the shooting started and rode up there, and someone shot my horse from under me. I got a good look at him, although I didn't recognise him, but I'll know his horse again."

"You're lying, Larew," one of the cowboys said bitterly. "You've thrown in your hand with Sutton."

"Did you see who stopped the second slug?" John Larew demanded. "Take a look across the yard and see who is lying on the porch."

They raised themselves and peered across the yard, and recognised Wire Sutton. The rancher had managed to crawl on to the porch.

"One of us nailed that skunk," someone said.

"I'm telling you that the ambusher shot him," Larew went. "The first shot got your boss, the second took Sutton. Does that sound like one of Sutton's crew shooting at you?"

"Why are the Broken S firing at us then?"

"Because you opened up at them." Larew started to

push himself to his feet. "Just stay down for a moment and I'll put a stop to this."

"You can't stick your nose out there. They'll cut you down."

"Someone's got to stop it," John Larew retorted firmly. "I'm thinking that Ben Lazzard played a mighty cunning trick around here. He had that waterhole poisoned, knowing that Clanton would bring his outfit here. So he put a man in position to start the shooting, in case it didn't come naturally. You must remember that Lazzard didn't know my brother learned of the poisoning part of the plot. He didn't know you would be riding in here as friends. If you hadn't been so quick on the trigger this could have been avoided."

"Okay," he was told. "Try and stop the Broken S from shooting and we'll talk this out. If Lazzard is behind this there's gonna be hell to pay on the Lazy L when we get there."

John Larew nodded and stood up. He moved forward until he could stare into the yard. Slugs whined about him, but he ignored the shooting. He lifted his hands high and stepped out into the open, walking forward slowly to where the majority of the Broken S crew were lying low in the barn and the bunkhouse. He was recognised, and the shooting petered out. As he reached the barn the echoes finally died away.

"What the hell you doing coming from them skunks?" someone demanded.

"They didn't start the shooting," Larew said. "The first shot came from the top of that slope over there."

"Must have been one of Clanton's men. Clanton would play it like that, putting a man in cover to ambush us."

"Did you see where the first slug struck?" Larew demanded.

"Yeah," another said. "It hit Clanton, and the second one hit our boss."

"So that proves it wasn't one of Clanton's men up there. Now put away your guns. There's been too much shooting. Ben Lazzard arranged for this, I've no doubt, and by the looks of it he's figured right. Let's take a look at the wounded. Then we'd better ride into Rainbow Creek like we planned. We don't know what's going on around there."

Larew walked out into the open again, and after some hesitation the Broken S cowboys put up their guns and followed him. Across the yard the Circle C outfit appeared, and for a moment both factions stood staring suspiciously. Larew started for the spot where Whisky Clanton was lying, and by the time he reached the still figure the two outfits were converging and moving towards him. There were seven men unwounded, and they began to check their more unfortunate pards.

Clanton was not dead, Larew saw. The rancher was hit bad, and seemed to be in a poor way, but he was still breathing. Larew went on to the house, and saw that Sutton was conscious, both hands pressed to his left side.

"Glad you got them off shooting," he said through clenched teeth as Larew reached him. "The damn fools! They played right into Lazzard's hands."

"Mebbe it was your fault," John Larew said. "Mebbe you should have expected something like that. You knew when you learned about the waterhole being poisoned that Lazzard expected Clanton to ride in here breathing fire and brimstone, so you should have considered that Lazzard would have sent a gunman along to stir things up."

"I guess so, but it's too late to consider that now," Sutton said weakly. "How bad is it over there?"

"Clanton's still alive, but there are some dead cowboys." Larew bent over the inert rancher and lifted the bloodstained hands away from the wound. He shook his head. This looked bad. "You're hit hard, Wire, but you're better off than Clanton. We'd better get you and the other wounded into the house, then ride fast for town. We'll have to get the Doc out here as soon as we can."

He straightened and turned to check the two crews, and found them mingling now. Clanton was being lifted and brought to the house, and some of Sutton's men came to attend to their boss. John Larew waited impatiently, and when order was restored he detailed a couple of men to stay with the wounded; one man from each outfit, and told the rest to get their horses.

"I didn't recognise the hombre who started all this shooting," he said tersely. "But I sure as hell will know his horse when I see it again. Come on, let's get moving. We better head for town, and the sooner we get there the better. Ben Lazzard is there, and we'll teach him a thing or two."

The cowboys needed no urging, and they quickly found their horses and mounted. John Larew looked around the yard as he set his horse into motion. This shooting had been a dreadful incident, and the man responsible was on the end of a shortening rope. It looked like a showdown was looming on the trail, and these half a dozen grim cowboys would help him make it come right against the Lazy L. They swept out of the yard and rode in the direction of the distant town. . . .

CHAPTER 7

"Now you're my deputy and it's official," Wickup said to Buck. "So let's get to work. What should we do first? How do we get on to the killer?"

"We'd better shift that crowd outside," Buck replied. "We can't do anything while they're shouting and creating a disturbance. You better go out and talk to them. Get them quieted down and then ask if anyone saw anything suspicious around town last night. Now all the men are together you won't have a better chance of talking to them."

"Good idea," the sheriff said, starting for the door. "Come on. You back me up in this and I got the feeling that we'll soon get it sorted out."

Buck smiled thinly as he followed the sheriff to the big front door. One of the men standing just inside turned and opened the door, and the sound of the many voices outside came swamping in like a physical blow against the ears. Buck grimaced as he stepped outside into the sunlight behind the sheriff. He caught Roan Morrell's eye, and saw surprise come to the cowboy's face when Morrell spotted the deputy badge on his chest. He grinned faintly, and nodded. Then he watched the sheriff trying to control the crowd, and stared around at the many excited faces. He saw Ben Lazzard and the gunman Drago Heppell, and his eyes narrowed. Neither man was showing any expression, but there was a certain eagerness in Lazzard's face that attracted Buck.

What had happened last night to drag the rancher out of his bed and take him along the trail in breakneck fashion? Why hadn't Lazzard gone all the way back to his ranch? Why had he returned to town before dawn? Buck figured that he should get the rancher to talk, but he knew that straight questions to Lazzard would only arouse the man's suspicions. There was another way to handle it, and he figured that the sheriff should attempt it.

The crowd was falling silent, although many of the men at the rear were still shouting for information. But finally there was silence on the street. Buck kept his eyes moving around the faces, looking for guilt. If the killer was here he would be hoping to learn what the law knew about the crime. Buck felt his blood race a little faster as he allowed his mind to delve into his own past experiences at law dealing. He had learned a lot in the Rangers, and his long training would help out here.

"Listen, men," Wickup shouted in harsh tones. "You all know what happened here during the night. Someone broke into the bank and killed Anders and cleaned out the big safe. I want you all to think about last night. Did anyone see or hear anything suspicious around town? Think hard. There might be some detail that you probably didn't think anything about at the time, but now you know about this you might begin to figure there was something suspicious. I'm going along to the jail right now, and if any of you thinks he might have seen the killers, or can throw any light upon this, then I want you to come along there, and soon."

There was a lot of talk among the men standing on the street, and Wickup turned to Buck.

"I'll leave Lee Paine here while you and I go along to the office. Do you know Lee, Buck? He's been my deputy for some time. Lee, meet Buck Larew."

The deputy studied Buck keenly, and he nodded soberly in reply to Buck's greeting. Paine had found the dead banker, and the shock of his experience was still showing in his face.

"Stick around here, Lee," Wickup said. "Don't let anyone into the bank. I'm just gonna take a walk around town and talk to a few people. I'll send the undertaker in here and he'll take care of the body."

The sheriff started along the sidewalk, and Buck began to follow. Morrell came to his side, and Buck halted.

"What's all that in aid of?" the Broken S cowboy demanded, poking a forefinger against the glinting star on Buck's chest.

"I figured it was the best thing to do in the circumstances," Buck replied. "It's given me some authority, and I'll be right on hand if anything goes wrong around here when our outfits show up."

"What do you make about this business then?" the cowboy went on.

"Nothing yet, but I've got some mighty nasty suspicions floating in my mind." Buck glanced around. He saw the sheriff still walking along to the law office. "Listen, Roan, and get this good. I'm wondering what Lazzard and his gunmen were doing riding through the night like we saw them. And they were back in the hotel around dawn. If they are guilty of this robbery and murder it's gonna take some proving. We can't accuse them openly, and we don't want to arouse their suspicions. I'm gonna get the sheriff to try something in a minute, and that'll give me a pointer in the right direction. But I want you to keep an eye on Lazzard and Heppell. Let's hope they'll stick together. But if they robbed the bank they'll surely do that. They won't lose sight of each other. You said last night that Lazzard did not have time to get to the Lazy L and back here again in the time he was out. So you know what I think? If they are guilty they had that dough with them last night when we saw them, and they took it somewhere to hide it."

"I get it," Morrell broke in quickly. "You figure they're gonna hang around here for a little while, then ride out to pick up the dough. Okay, I'm your man. You do what you can around here and I'll trail those two. If they have got that dough stashed away some place then I'll be on their tails when they go to pick it up."

"Good. I'll see you around, and if I learn anything at all I'll drop by and have a word with you. I'd better go now. The sheriff is about ready to start running around in circles. I want to put a curb on him."

He slapped Morrell on the shoulder and left the cowboy. As he followed the sheriff he glanced around and saw that Lazzard and his gunman were moving away from the crowd, heading back towards the hotel.

In the sheriff's office Wickup was pacing up and down. The worry that stained the lawman's leathery cheeks made Buck shake his head. It was a good thing for the whole county that Buck Larew had shown up when he did, he thought. He entered the office and closed the door at his back. Wickup glanced at him.

"We're never gonna find the killer," the sheriff complained. "Where the hell do we start?"

"I'll tell you," Buck retorted. "But it's got to be handled carefully in case we give the men any suspicions that we're on to them."

"What the hell are you talking about?" Wickup demanded, his blue eyes showing surprise. "Do you mean to tell me that you've already got hold of some clue?"

"I'm half sure that I got a clue last night and didn't know it at the time," Buck retorted, and the sheriff's jaw dropped in surprise. He grinned tightly, and told the sheriff how Roan Morrell had recognised Lazzard in the

dark as the two riders had passed them. He went on to
say that after taking the room at the hotel they had
checked Lazzard's room and found it unoccupied, also
Heppell's.

"But why should you be suspicious of Lazzard then?"
the sheriff demanded. "You didn't know about the
robbery then."

Buck told him what had happened out on the range,
how he had sneaked into the Lazy L and overheard the
foreman declare that the waterhole on Clanton's range
had been poisoned, with the object of causing shooting
trouble between the Circle C and the Broken S.

"God Almighty!" Wickup said, his eyes wide with
shock, and there was despair seeping into his face. "How
the hell are we gonna cope with all this? I've known for
a long time that things haven't been right on the range
around here. But there was no proof against anyone. I
knew someone was stirring things up. Now you tell me
it was Lazzard. Well I can believe it, but Ben Lazzard
is a mighty smart hombre. How in hell are we gonna get
proof against him?"

"Don't panic," Buck said. "I've got Roan Morrell
watching Ben Lazzard and the gunman. If they should
head out of town Morrell will follow them, and we'll
soon know for certain if they did ride out last night to
hide that stolen dough. Now there is something you can
do right now which will help."

"Anything," Wickup said. "Just so long as we can
get a grip on this trouble and solve it without more shooting and bloodshed."

"I want you to start asking questions of some of the
townsmen, and include Lazzard. When you get to
Lazzard tell him that you're questioning every man in
the town, and ask him if he saw anything suspicious, like
you just asked the whole crowd back there. Then ask him

when he went to bed last night. If he's guilty as I suspect he's gonna deny being out of his room at any time during the night."

"What happens if he does lie? Do we arrest him?"

"Nope. We give him enough rope to hang himself," Buck replied. "Now you better get started. If this is like I've got it figured then Lazzard will soon be making tracks out of town."

"He told me last evening that he was staying the night, and pulling out this morning," Wickup remarked. "Come to think of it Ben Lazzard was acting suspiciously on the street last night." He told Buck about his encounter in the darkened alley with the Lazy L rancher.

"Could be something in it," Buck replied. "Lazzard will surely need checking on, Sheriff."

"You better come along with me, just in case," Wickup said. "I don't want to be on my own in case Lazzard is guilty and my questions scare him into shooting. You're a good man with a gun?"

"Tolerable," Buck replied. "I spent five years along the border down in Texas, and I'm still alive to talk about it."

"Heard that was mighty rough country," Wickup said. He heaved a sigh and started for the door, and Buck followed the lawman out to the sunny street.

There were still a lot of men around the street, and they were standing in small groups discussing the robbery and murder. Wickup paused and looked around, and heaved another long sigh. He caught Buck's eye, and shrugged.

"This is sure gonna leave its mark on the county," he said.

"There's more to come," Buck replied. "I told you that the Broken S and the Circle C will be riding in. They're gonna want an accounting with Lazzard. Our only hope is that Lazzard won't head for home too soon and meet up with Sutton and Clanton on the way."

"We better get moving," the sheriff retorted determinedly. "Let's go look for Lazzard."

"He was heading back for the hotel when I last saw him," Buck said. "He might be preparing to leave right now."

They went across the street and walked along the crowded sidewalk towards the hotel. Men kept calling to them for news, but Wickup did no more than shrug. They reached the hotel, and Buck spotted Morrell seated on the bench outside. He told the sheriff to wait inside for him, and moved to the cowboy's side and dropped down with a sigh.

"We're now gonna brace Lazzard," Buck said to Morrell. "No shooting or anything like that. I want to test him out, hear what he's got to say about certain things. You stay here in case he decides to leave town quick."

"Okay," the cowboy told him. "But you watch out for that Heppell. He's mighty fast with his hogleg."

"We'll handle it," Buck said. "Now if you do have to trail them out of town be content to watch them. Don't tangle with them, or give them any reason to get suspicious."

"You can leave that part of it to me," Morrell said. "I shan't let you down."

Buck nodded and got to his feet. He stepped into the hotel and found the sheriff waiting for him. As they approached the reception desk Buck spotted Ben Lazzard and Heppell coming down the stairs. Lazzard spotted them and narrowed his eyes as he came across.

"Dreadful thing happened there in the bank," the Lazy L rancher said tightly. "I hope you get the ones who did it, Bub."

"Yeah, me too," the sheriff replied. "You pulling out, Ben?"

"Yeah. I told you last night I was riding back to my place this morning."

"Well I better ask you a few questions before you leave," the sheriff went on. "I'm asking every man who was in town last night if he saw or heard anything that might have been the killer. I remember that I saw you on the street."

"Yeah, so you did," Lazzard said easily. "But just after I left you I went back to the hotel and turned in. I didn't see or hear a thing until the sun came up this morning and Drago came hammering on my door."

"Uhuh." Wickup did not change expression. "About what time was it you got to bed then?"

"I don't know exactly. I reckon it was about ten." The rancher paused. "Is there anything else, Bub? I got a long ride ahead."

"Nope. But I must ask Heppell the same question. What about it? What time did you go to bed? Did you see anything suspicious around town at any time after ten?"

"Not me," Heppell replied. "I went up to my room early. You can check that with the night clerk. I spoke to him on my way in. I got into bed and stayed there all night. I'm a heavy sleeper. The sun was up when I stirred."

"No need to check up on anything," Wickup said. "Hell, I ain't got no suspicions on anyone like you and Ben. It's the riff-raff around here that I got to get to work on."

"We'll get moving then," Lazzard said. "If you happen to see my son around this morning you might tell him that I've headed back to the ranch."

"Sure," the sheriff retorted. "If he's in town then I'll

certainly see him. I'm questioning every last man around."

"Rather you than me," Lazzard retorted. "So long."

He continued on his way with the gunman following, and Buck stared after the pair of them. Lazzard was lying, and that was very promising. Wickup waited until the two had gone out the door before turning to Buck. There was a bright light in the lawman's pale blue eyes.

"Well?" he demanded eagerly. "What do you make of that? They both lied, didn't they?"

"They sure did," Buck replied, nodding his head slowly. "I know for a fact that they were on the trail during the small hours. But don't you worry about a thing. I reckon Morrell will find out what they're up to. Still, now we've got something more than suspicion to work on I think I'd better play this safe. I think I ought to trail Morrell, Sheriff. If Lazzard is guilty he ain't gonna take any chances, and I shouldn't want him to catch Morrell on his trail."

"Okay, so you want to ride out. Do you think you'd better take some men along with you?"

"Nope. There's only Lazzard and his gunman. Morrell will stick with them, and I reckon I could hold my own against them in any circumstances, so we'll handle this quietly. If they have cached the dough and we see them pick it up I'll arrest them and bring them back to town."

"I hope it goes like you plan," Wickup said. "But what should I do around town?"

"Clean up the mess and keep asking around like you have done. Someone might have seen something, and if Lazzard is guilty but intends playing this smart by leaving the dough hidden for a time then we're gonna have to try other means of getting at the truth. Don't ask me how yet. I don't have any idea. All I know is that Ben Lazzard is a mighty clever man."

"You can say that again. But take it easy out there. If you give him any reason for suspicion he'll turn out his crew, and they're a real tough bunch."

"Don't worry about me," Buck said. "I'll see you later."

He left the hotel and peered along the street towards the stable. He thought he saw Morrell, but there were so many men standing around that he couldn't get a clear view. He started along the sidewalk, threading his way through the groups and ignoring the curious stares that were directed at him and his badge. The county would soon get to know him, he thought grimly, and that went for the men stirring up all the trouble.

He slowed his pace as he neared the stable, and waited in the shade until he saw Ben Lazzard and Drago Heppell ride out. The two horsemen headed out of town without looking left or right, and Buck smiled grimly to himself and entered the stable, to find Roan Morrell hurriedly saddling up.

"Roan, I'm gonna sit on your tail," Buck said, and relief showed itself on the cowboy's face. "You trail those two carefully, and I'll keep you in sight. Between us we oughta be able to handle this. But a word of warning. Ben Lazzard is a smart hombre, and if he has got that bank money cached somewhere around then you can bet your boots that he ain't gonna take any chances with it."

"Okay," Morrell said. "I'll tag along and see what happens. If they head straight back to the Lazy L I'll see you out there, and you can decide what to do after."

"Leave it like that," Buck said. "Now you better get moving. Don't take any chances."

Morrell nodded, and grinned despite his harshly set face. He climbed into his saddle and rode out, and Buck turned to the stall where his own mount was standing. He prepared for travel and then led the horse outside.

He didn't want to get too close to Morrell, and he knew which way the cowboy was riding. They had been some miles out of town when they spotted Lazzard and his gunman the night before.

The stableman appeared, carrying a pitchfork, and Buck trailed his reins and crossed to the man.

"Howdy," he greeted. "I'd like to have a word with you."

"Sure," the man agreed, sticking the fork into a pile of litter. "What can I do for you? You're a stranger around here, ain't you? Are you with the local law or from some place out of town?"

"I'm with your local department," Buck said. "I'm Buck Larew, brother of John, who owns the Bar Sixty."

"Glad to know you, Larew. Your brother is a good man. What can I do to help you?"

"Ben Lazzard and Drago Heppell just rode out," Buck said. "Can you tell me if their horses were hard ridden during the night?"

"They weren't as a matter of fact," the stableman retorted. "I usually take a walk around first thing to check up. I live opposite, you see, and the barn is left open to all comers during the night."

"Are you sure they hadn't been out since Lazzard and Heppell put them in yesterday?"

"Can't say for sure. Didn't look that close. They hadn't been run hard, and that's all I can tell you."

"Okay, thanks." Buck turned away and went back to his horse. He gathered up the reins and climbed into the saddle. There was nothing for it but to ride out. He had wanted confirmation that Lazzard and the gunman had ridden out during the night, although both the rancher and Heppell had condemned themselves by claiming that they hadn't left their rooms all night.

He loped along the street, raising dust, and soon left

town. He kept to a canter, knowing that he had to keep well back. If anything went wrong he wanted to remain out of sight, although it was risking Morrell's life. But for the first part of his ride Morrell had every right to be on the trail. The Broken S lay in this direction. The turn off was several miles ahead.

The miles slid by and Buck began to feel the heat. He kept looking ahead with anxiety throbbing inside him. If Lazzard and Heppell should ride into Sutton and Clanton there would be hell to pay. He hoped it wouldn't come to that. The longer open warfare was held off the better chance there was that this could be settled without bloodshed.

Several times he caught a glimpse of Roan Morrell ahead, and he closed upon the cowboy a little, afraid that he would be too far away to help Morrell if Heppell or Lazzard spotted him. Morrell didn't turn in his saddle. The man seemed to know something about tracking. He wasn't taking his eyes off his quarry.

Buck was more than half certain that Lazzard and his pet gunman were responsible for the robbery and murder, but he knew it would be difficult to prove. The easiest way of getting the evidence would be to catch Lazzard and Heppell picking up the money from the spot where it had been cached. But Buck did not depend upon lucky breaks. He had been a lawman too long to rely upon that method of solving crimes. It would have to be done the hard way, with plenty of riding and watching to help it.

He closed on Morrell as the morning wore away. Now they were at the spot beyond which Lazzard and Heppell could not have passed last night. The two men had returned to the hotel in town just before dawn. That limited the distance they could have covered. If they had hidden the money around here then they would have to stop and pick it up. He pushed his horse on faster. He wanted to be with Morrell if that happened. They could take the two redhanded.

Morrell had vanished over a crest ahead, and Buck rode cautiously. He dismounted before he reached the crest and trailed his reins, walking up the rest of the way, and dropping flat before he got on the skyline. He slithered forward then and eased himself into a position of observation. A frown came to his tanned face when he failed to spot Morrell anywhere ahead. The trail stretched away down the slope and continued for a couple of miles in plain view. There was no sign of Morrell or the men the cowboy had been following.

Buck let his eyes scan the foreground. There was a grove of trees about four hundred yards ahead, to the right of the trail. Apart from that there didn't seem to be any cover around. There were plenty of hillocks and depressions, but he didn't figure that Lazzard would drop into one of those, unless the rancher was playing it smart and had got into cover to watch for anyone who might be following. But if that had happened Morrell wouldn't have crossed the crest. He would have laid low until Lazzard moved on again. Unless he figured that the two men he was following had gone into the grove to pick up their loot.

There was no movement anywhere ahead, and Buck forced patience into his heart and lay still, content to watch. If Morrell had walked into trouble it was likely that Lazzard and Heppell were watching the trail to see if there was a second tracker. Minutes passed and there was rising concern in Buck's mind. What had happened to Morrell? The cowboy knew that he was being trailed. And where were the two suspects? If they were riding for the Lazy L they should have stuck to the trail, and they would have been in plain view even now.

Buck eased forward a little more and looked for tracks. He could see the prints left by Morrell's horse, and they led down the slope, but he couldn't see far enough ahead from this position to note where they turned off the trail or in which direction they went.

He let more time elapse. He would be a prize fool to ride out into the open and get himself spotted by Lazzard. But he couldn't help wondering if Morrell had fallen into their unscrupulous hands. They might be murdering the cowboy right now. Buck thinned his lips and tried to stop his imagination. He wouldn't be able to do anything at this moment, except jeopardise the whole situation.

His eyes began to ache, staring into the glare of the sun. There was a shimmering heat haze across the middle distance, and he slowly studied every foot of the ground. He saw nothing that indicated the presence of men down there. When he could stand the suspense no longer he pushed himself back from the crest and went down for his horse. He climbed in the saddle and gigged the animal forward, riding over the crest and down the reverse slope. He didn't turn his head to look around, but his brown eyes were busy.

At the bottom of the slope he paused to look for tracks, and saw recent sign. He lifted his eyes and studied the direction of the tracks, and nodded to himself when they cut off towards the trees. He began to ride, and now he was tense and doubly alert. His right hand stayed close to the butt of his Colt, and there was a tightening of the muscles in his throat. His chest felt constricted.

He turned off, following the tracks, and rode for the trees, watching for the slightest movement that would warn of the presence of a waiting man. He looked for the glint of sunlight on metal, and was keyed up to leap from the saddle at the first sign of ambush. But nothing happened. The silence was intense, apart from the noises of his movements; the harsh breathing of his horse and the creak of saddle leather. He rode into the trees, squinting around into the thick shadows and undergrowth. He saw nothing. He reined up and slid out of the saddle, his right hand caressing the butt of his Colt. He trailed his reins and walked around, peering about for sign of Morrell or the two men the cowboy had been following.

When he came to a screen of bushes he tightened his lips and moved around them, and saw instantly a narrow ravine cutting down into the ground, running deeply down a shelving slope, and at a broken spot on the left hand wall there were marks where a horse had scrambled down into the deep cover. Buck stared for a moment, then nodded to himself. That ravine had not been visible from the crest, and it stretched away into broken country. This was the way Lazzard and Heppell had gone, and judging by the sign on the ground, Morrell was hot on their trails.

Buck went back for his horse and mounted. He rode back to the ravine and set the animal at the sharp decline. They reached the bottom amid a shower of small stones and dislodged earth, and Buck eased his gun in its holster as he continued. The ravine wound lazily down the slope, and there was plenty of sign that riders had passed through recently. He hoped that Morrell was using plenty of caution.

The walls of the ravine began to climb higher about him, and Buck felt dwarfed and hemmed in. He sat forward in his saddle, peering ahead for sign of Morrell, and he was wondering what Lazzard and Heppell were doing down here, off their trail to the Lazy L. The next instant he reached a bend in the ravine, where it twisted with the changing ground above, and as he rounded the obstacle he spotted Morrell just ahead. The cowboy was sitting his mount, his hands raised shoulder high, and Lazzard and Heppell were confronting him, their guns drawn and levelled.

Buck tried to rein up, but Heppell spotted his movement, and the gunman flicked the muzzle of his gun to cover Buck, who made a fast draw almost before he realized that he was doing so. He palmed his Colt as Morrell spurred his mount. The horse blundered into Heppell's horse, causing it to rear, and the gunman lost his aim. Lazzard started shouting at the top of his voice, no doubt in the hope that his words would throw Buck off aim. But Buck was an old hand, and he swung up his Colt, his thumb earing back the hammer. Morrell's horse continued across the front of Heppell, and the gunman was striving to control his plunging animal. Then Heppell's gun exploded deafeningly, hurling echoes into the rocks. Morrell swayed in his saddle, kicked his feet clear of the stirrups, and fell sideways to the ground.

Buck sent a shot at Heppell, and saw the gunman jerk under the impact of the heavy slug. But it was only a glancing hit, and Buck knew that. He thumbed back his hammer for a second shot, gritting his teeth when he saw that Lazzard was levelling his sixgun. The rancher's weapon exploded then, and as Buck sent his second shot at Heppell he felt the impact of Lazzard's slug. It was like the kick of a mule against his chest. Pain flashed through him like the stab of a sharp knife. He gasped and gripped the barrel of his horse with his knees. He dropped the reins from his left hand and concentrated upon getting his gun to bear upon Lazzard. Heppell was low in his saddle, and still trying to get his gun into the aim. Buck fired at Lazzard, and the rancher whirled his horse away, swinging in behind an outcrop of obdurate rock. Heppell fired again, and his slug caught Buck's skull a glancing blow.

Lightning flashed in Buck's mind, and blackness clawed through him. He swayed in his saddle, feeling his senses going, and he had just enough sense left to free his feet of the stirrups before he went out of the saddle and lost consciousness.

CHAPTER 8

JOHN LAREW decided upon the shortest route to Rainbow Creek, and he didn't spare his horse on the ride. The half dozen cowboys following him were grimfaced and determined. They pushed on fast, raising dust, and they were silent and resolute. Each man was thinking about the wounded cowboys and ranchers, and there wasn't one among them who didn't curse Ben Lazzard for the murderous plot that had been laid. Their hoofs thundered on the hard ground, and they crossed rough range, heading towards the distant town. It would be some hours before the doctor got out to the Sutton place, and by then Clanton might be dead.

Larew kept his eyes skinned as he rode, not forgetting the man who had started the shooting back at the ranch, and when he spotted a small cloud of dust far ahead he twisted in his saddle and called to the cowboys.

"Someone's ahead of us," he snapped. "Could be the man who started the shooting. Let's catch up with him and see who he is."

The cowboys needed no urging, and they redoubled their efforts to get the best speed out of their willing mounts. Larew maintained his lead, and they swept forward, slowly gaining on the dust ahead.

Thirty minutes later John Larew got his first glimpse of the rider, and recognised the horse immediately. He turned and told the cowboys. They whooped, and some of them drew their guns.

"No shooting," John Larew shouted. "We want him alive. We don't know for certain that Lazzard was behind it. Let's take him and make him talk."

They continued, and drew even closer to the un-suspecting rider. Then the thunder of their approaching hoofs reached the man, and he twisted in his saddle, his dark face showing instant fear.

"It's Pete Roscoe," one of the cowboys yelled.

John Larew had heard the name, and associated it with the lawless element. Roscoe had almost been jailed some months before for attempted rustling. That much he knew, and as the man ahead spurred his horse to make a run for it, Larew pulled his gun.

"Hold up there, Roscoe," he yelled, "or we'll cut you down."

One of the cowboys fired a couple of shots into the air, but the shooting only served to scare the gunman into flight. He kicked his horse into a fast run, and John Larew pulled a face. But they could run him down. The next instant Roscoe was pitching sideways out of his saddle. He hit the ground hard, rolled, then lay still. Larew thought for a moment that one of the cowboys had shot the gunman, but there was no sound of a gun firing.

They reined up in a circle around the fallen figure, and Larew and two of the others dismounted. Larew bent over Roscoe and stared at the man's pale face. Roscoe was unconscious. He had fallen badly, and his left leg was crumpled awkwardly under him. There was blood on his forehead where he had come into contact with a piece of rock.

"Is he dead?" someone demanded.

"Nope, still breathing," John Larew said. "Anyone got a water canteen with him?"

One of the cowboys handed over a canteen, and Larew uncorked it and dribbled some water on the unconscious man's face. One of the other riders went off for Roscoe's horse, and came back with it moments later.

"This is the man who did the shooting from ambush," John Larew said. "I recognise his figure and his clothes, and I'd know the horse anywhere."

"Bring him to his senses so we can question him. Then we'll finish him off."

"Don't be silly," Larew warned. "If he was sent out there by Ben Lazzard then we'll need him in court to give evidence."

They were silent as Larew worked on Roscoe. Moments passed, and then the gunman opened his eyes. He stared up at the grim faces looking down at him, and he recognised some of them. His eyes narrowed, and a cunning light appeared in them, but pain inside Roscoe drove all thoughts of guile out of him. He closed his eyes and groaned.

"Roscoe," Larew said. "You're the man who shot Whisky Clanton and Wire Sutton this morning, and you damn near got me when I came after you. Who paid you to handle that chore?"

"I don't know what you mean," the gunman replied. "I'm a mighty sick man. I think I'm dying."

"What's wrong with you?"

"Been ill for weeks. Belly pains. Was in bed until early today. Haven't been out for a week."

"You're gonna wish you stayed at home today," one of the punchers retorted.

"Take me into Rainbow Creek," Roscoe said. "I got to see the Doc. I think I'm gonna croak."

"We got some men out at the Broken S who are waiting to see the Doc," one of the cowboys said. "You better come across with the truth or you'll die pronto. Who paid you to ambush us out at the Broken S?"

"No one paid me anything," the gunman replied.

"Okay, if that's the way you wanta play it," someone said. "There's a tree over there. I'll get my rope and build a noose in it. If he wants to play it tough than so can we."

"I'm a sick man," Roscoe said harshly. His pleading eyes turned to John Larew. "Don't let them go through with this," he gasped. "Can't you see I'm dying?"

"You'll be dead before we ride on," he was told grimly.

"I reckon we better tote him into town and hand him over to the law," Larew said. "If he is ill he's gotta see the Doc."

"Yeah, and when they've cured him they better take him out and hang him high," one of the cowboys snapped. "If I catch him around this county again I'll put a bullet through his heart."

"Get me on my hoss," Roscoe said. "It's gonna be touch and go. I can feel it inside."

"You better die and get it over with, and save the county the expense of giving you a trial and hanging you."

"There ain't nothing you can pin on me," Roscoe muttered.

"I recognised you," John Larew told him, beckoning to one of the others to give him a hand. They lifted Roscoe and thrust him none too gently into his saddle. "That'll be good enough in any law court to get the rope put around your neck."

"You're making a big mistake," Roscoe said, slumping in his saddle. "But you can talk later. For God's sake get me into town and let the Doc take a look at me."

They mounted up, and with Roscoe safely in the centre of their group they went on. Now they felt easier. They had the man who had ambushed them, and by the time they got him to town he would be ready to talk. The heat from the sun boiled down on them, and John Larew was sweating freely. He kept wiping his forehead on his sleeve, and kept a wary eye on Pete Roscoe. He had figured that the gunman was maybe shamming his illness in order to get them to relax their vigilance, but as they progressed he could see that the gunman was ill. But they kept pushing on, and they didn't let up until Roscoe suddenly fell sideways out of his saddle. The gunman hit the ground hard, and two of the following riders galloped over him. Larew cursed and hauled his mount to a halt. He stepped to the ground and went running back to where Roscoe lay, and shook his head when he dropped to one knee beside the gunman. Roscoe was in a real bad way. He straightened and turned to face the riders who had turned and were coming back.

"Mebbe we better leave him here with someone to watch him," he said. "I reckon he ain't well enough to continue. We'll push on, and get a wagon to come out and pick him up."

There was some argument, but at length they all agreed that Roscoe should stay where he was with a cowboy to guard him. Blankets were handed down to Larew, and he made the sick man as comfortable as possible. One of the cowboys off-saddled and sighed as he sat down in the shade, and the rest of them continued.

It was mid morning when they sighted Rainbow Creek, and John Larew heaved a great sigh of relief as he entered the wide street. He twisted in his saddle and spoke to the cowboys.

"One of you head for the stable and get a wagon moving out," he commanded. "Another go see the Doc, and tell him about Roscoe and what happened at the Broken S. We'll meet again at the law office. We might have some cleaning up to do around here."

"Ben Lazzard?" one of the cowboys demanded.

"We'll hear what my brother has to report before we make any decisions," John Larew said grimly.

Two of the cowboys went off to carry out their errands, and Larew led the other four towards the sheriff's office. They dismounted and tied their mounts to the rail at the edge of the sidewalk, and the cowboys relaxed on the sidewalk while Larew entered the office.

Bub Wickup was seated at his desk, staring down at some sheets of paper which were before him. He sighed as he looked up at John Larew, but his grin of welcome died when he read Larew's expression.

"What's wrong?" he demanded.

Larew told him, omitting nothing, and he finished up with a description of how they had come upon the sick Pete Roscoe. The sheriff's bleak face showed a whole procession of fleeting emotions as he listened, and when John Larew lapsed into silence the lawman got to his feet and came from behind his desk. He began to pace the floor.

"Is my brother around?" John Larew demanded.

The sheriff halted his pacing and stared at Larew. He shook his head. Larew misconstrued the lawman's motion. He thinned his lips.

"Nothing's happened to Buck, has there?" he demanded. "He didn't go after Lazzard by himself, did he?"

Wickup paused for a moment, then began a terse narrative of what had been happening around town. It was Larew's turn to show surprise, and he took a deep breath and heaved a sigh when the sheriff described how Buck had become a deputy and taken out after Lazzard and Heppell.

"I'd better get these cowboys together and take out after him," Larew said. "I ain't running any risk of losing Buck now. You know what a tough bunch Lazzard runs. Why didn't you get a posse to take out after him?"

"Because that would ruin everything," the sheriff said. "We ain't got no proof against Lazzard. Your brother is a mighty smart hombre, and he's working on an idea that should pin the guilt where it belongs."

"If he doesn't get himself killed," John Larew said. "I don't like it, Sheriff. You better get a posse together and moving out of town, just in case. There's about a score of gunmen on Lazzard's payroll. Buck can't fight the whole bunch of them."

"He's not fool enough to try," Wickup said. "But I will get some men together and warn them to stand by for posse duty."

"I'll tell these cowboys to stick around, and we'll all ride out together," John Larew said, heading for the door. "But there's one thing I've got to do before I leave. I want to see Letty Haig."

"Ike Lazzard is around, John," Wickup said. "You better watch your step."

"I've had enough of the warnings that have been pushed at me about seeing Letty," Larew said. "I'm gonna get my affairs straightened out once and for all. It's about time I came to my senses. I've been a blamed fool, acting the way I did. But that was when the Lazzards had all the power around here. Right now it looks as if they're through."

"Don't be too sure about that," the sheriff warned. "I wouldn't count on Lazzard getting pinned for this. He's a smart one."

John Larew went out. There were some townsmen gathering to talk to the cowboys, and Larew pushed his way through them. He asked the cowboys to stand by to ride with the posse, and they were all for it. He turned away and started along the sidewalk, and he was cold inside. He wanted to see Letty Haig. He was in love with the girl, and he had let the situation rob him of his

courage and his self-respect. But that was done with
now. If he wanted to hold up his head around here after
the trouble was over then he had to make some kind of
play. He had to earn his rights.

He reached the store where Letty worked during the
day, and paused on the sidewalk. He looked around.
There were still groups of men talking about the robbery and the killing. It was a nine days' wonder! He
smiled grimly. There would be a lot more to talk about
before this was finally settled. He entered the big
store.

It was gloomy inside the building, and his nostrils
were assailed by the conglomeration of aromas that came
from the many brands of merchandise. He looked
around. There were several women standing at the long
counter, waiting to be served, and his heart almost missed
a beat when he spotted the tall figue of Ike Lazzard
propped against the far end of the store. Lazzard looked
up as Larew's shadow darkened the doorway, and when
he recognised Larew he came erect and shrugged his
heavy shoulders.

John Larew took a slow breath and moved into the
store. He wanted to talk to Letty, and no spoiled brat
of a rich father was going to stop him. Ike Lazzard had
never done a hard day's work in his life. He had never
been fated to toil for what he had. He had ridden rough-
shod around the county, and got away with it because
his father had money and power and a salty crew.

But times were changing. The threat of retaliation by
a whole crew had prevented most local men from making
any kind of a stand against the Lazy L boss and his son.
Now there was a posse forming to ride out to the Lazy L,
and there would likely be shooting before it was ended.

Ike Lazzard came forward a couple of yards, and set
his shoulders truculently. When he spoke his voice

cracked harshly above the muttering voices of the women.

"What the hell are you doing in here, Larew?" the youngster demanded, and Larew thinned his lips at the insolence that was laid bare in the tones. But Ike Lazzard was overlooking the fact that for once he didn't have any of his father's pet gunmen around to back him up.

"And what the hell has that got to do with you?" Larew replied defiantly. He was as tall, and heavier, than the younger man. There was an edge to his tones that should have warned Lazzard, but the youngster was too set in his brash ways to care, or even notice that there was a change in John Larew.

"I'm making it my damned business," Lazzard said, coming forward again. "I'm marrying Letty in a couple of months, and no sneaking skunk like you is gonna come around when I ain't looking."

"You're looking now, Ike," Larew said through stiff lips. He did not move as the youngster halted within arm's length. "I got something to say to Letty, and it ain't for your ears."

"Over my dead body," Lazzard said thickly.

"Have it which way you like," Larew snapped, and struck quickly and viciously, with all his surging strength. His right hand closed as his knuckles crashed against Lazzard's jaw, and the youngster was hurled backwards by the force of the blow. One of the women customers screamed, and they all stampeded for the door. Letty Haig came through from a back room, carrying a bolt of cloth, and the girl halted in shock, fear flashing into her lovely face as she took in the situation.

"No, John," she cried, dropping the cloth and coming fast around the counter. Her blue eyes were wide with shock and consternation.

"Stay back, Letty," Larew warned, transferring his

attention back to the struggling Lazzard, who was flat
on his back and looking dazed. Larew narrowed his eyes.
"Get yourself on your feet and prove that you can handle
yourself like a man," he grated. "You've been running
around this county too long, shouting off your mouth
and getting away with everything short of murder because your father is Ben Lazzard. Well that's all a thing
of the past now, and it's about time someone taught you
a thing or two."

Lazzard came surging erect, cursing angrily, and he
clenched his fists and rushed Larew, who swayed to the
left and dealt the younger man a shrewd, heavy blow to
the stomach. Lazzard's swinging fist grazed the back of
John Larew's neck, and the rancher moved his feet to
maintain his balance, and struck again, using left and
right. The left fist drew blood from Lazzard's long nose,
and the right thudded into the body again, causing
Lazzard to wilt. Then they were mixing it, standing close
together and throwing everything they had. The sound
of knuckles pounding flesh was sickening, and the watching girl moved back, fascinated by the sight of two men
determined to beat each other to the ground.

Larew took some punishment, but he was a tough man
who had spent the better part of his working life in the
saddle of a cow pony, working all hours God made.
Lazzard was a waster who had never done a day's work
in his life, and the long hours of drinking and whoop-
ing it up had already taken their toll of his youthful
body.

Larew knocked Lazzard down again, and stood over
the youngster, taunting him, driving him to further
effort with his sharp tongue. There was a hardness in
Larew now that would brook no failure. He had taken a
lot from the two Lazzards and the Lazy L crew, but a
man could absorb only so much, and John Larew had

reached his limit. Now he was going to fight as hard as he knew.

Lazzard came shakily to his feet, wiping blood from his eyebrows. He charged in, head down, fists working like pistons, and Larew sidestepped and dealt out some heavy blows, his left fist smacking heavily in the younger man's face. The right was sledging in to the body, and now Lazzard was wilting at each blow, groaning as the heavy knuckles crashed against his shrinking flesh. His mouth was agape, and the sound of his heavy breathing was harsh, a sure sign that he was coming to a halt. He went spinning away from a heavy right hand to the jaw, and crashed across the counter and disappeared headfirst over the far side.

Larew halted and let his shoulders sag. He waited for Lazzard to come again, and saw the man's hands come up and take hold of the edge of the counter. Larew let his eyes slide to the watching girl's face, and saw the fear shining in her pale eyes. He grinned crookedly, and felt pain as his bottom lip split a little wider. He could taste the saltiness of his blood in his mouth, but he was happier than he had felt for a long time.

Lazzard came slowly to his feet and stood swaying. His face was smothered with blood. He was snuffling, and a fine red froth showed on his tightly drawn lips. He stared at Larew for a moment, then muttered something that was unintelligible. The next instant he had started his hand to the butt of his gun.

Letty Haig cried out in sudden fear, and Larew shouted a warning. But Ike Lazzard was deaf and blind to everything except the desire to kill. His gun cleared leather and he started shooting wildly. The first slug clipped the brim of Larew's Stetson, and the Bar Sixty rancher dived around a stack of crates and drew his own long barrelled Colt. He cocked the weapon, showing his teeth in a snarl as Lazzard emptied his Colt, filling the gloomy store with thunder and smoke. He counted the shots, and at the sixth he pushed himself around the crates, his gun levelled.

Lazzard was disappearing fast through the back door, dragging Letty Haig with him. Larew lifted his gun, then lowered it. Lazzard turned and glanced at him, spitting blood.

"You foller me and I'll kill her," he shouted, and the door banged shut behind him.

Larew hesitated for the barest moment, then he thinned his lips and moved in pursuit. He would settle this once and for all. Either Lazzard would kill him or he would make the bully eat crow, and that would be the end of Lazzard in these parts. If he came off second best he wouldn't dare show his face around. He reached the back door and peered outside, then ducked as Lazzard's gun cracked and the slug hammered into the door. He saw Lazzard moving away across the back lots, the girl still held close to him.

Larew didn't think Lazzard would harm the girl, unless he figured she might turn against him. There was a lot of meanness in Ike Lazzard. That would have to be let out of him before this was done, and it seemed that a bullet was the only way of accomplishing it. He slid out of the building and started in pursuit, watching Lazzard making for the stable. He followed resolutely, and kept going even when Lazzard turned and emptied his gun at him. But Lazzard was all shaken up, and his shooting was wild.

As Larew passed an alley mouth a couple of the punchers who had ridden in with him appeared at his elbow, and they demanded to know what was going on. They fell into step beside Larew, and he explained.

"Leave it to me," he suggested. "This is personal between me and Ike Lazzard."

"We'll string along to see nothing happens to the girl," one of the cowpokes said, and they went forward together.

Lazzard paused in the rear doorway of the barn, and started shooting again. The two cowboys ducked away, but Larew kept moving forward, intent upon coming up with the youngster. He heard the screeching slugs passing closely around him, but knew that Lazzard had to be lucky to score any kind of a hit. He was holding his gun ready, but he made no attempt to get in a shot. He dared not take the chance of hitting Letty.

Lazzard ducked back out of the doorway, and Larew kept moving. The two cowboys appeared at his side again, and they continued.

"Are you gonna kill him?" one of the punchers demanded.

"If he won't throw down the gun I shall," Larew replied.

They approached the barn, and Larew kept wide of the doorway, moving across it at a distance of twenty yards. The cowboys made for the nearest wall and stayed close to it.

Larew halted in plain view of the doorway. It was gloomy inside the barn, but he knew that Lazzard would be able to see him clearly. He held his gun down at his side, watching for movement inside. He heard a horse stamp, but saw nothing.

"Lazzard," he yelled. "Turn Letty loose and come on out. I'll fight you if that's what you want. You've shouted off your mouth long enough about what you'd do to me if you ever got the chance. Well now you've got it. Come on and let's see if you are a man. You've been trying to act like one long enough."

There was no reply, and Larew heaved a sigh. He stared into the barn, hoping to get a glimpse of Lazzard, but nothing moved. He started to pace forward, and now he lifted his gun and prepared to fight, but in the back of his mind was the fear that something might happen to Letty.

As he closed on the doorway the two cowboys inched forward from the side. They didn't look at Larew, and he dared not take his attention from the interior of the barn. He reached the doorway and peered inside, and caught sight of Letty Haig standing in a stall about half-way along the barn. The girl did not move, and her face showed fright.

"Stay out of it, John," she called. "He's gonna kill me if you try anything."

"That's right, Larew," Ike Lazzard yelled, although he did not show himself. "You better get outa here. I'm desperate now. If you don't want Letty to get hurt then beat it back where you came from."

"Hold it," Larew said to the cowboys. "He means what he says. Better stay back."

"We can wait it out," one of the men said. "He can't get away."

Larew was staring around, and he saw the ladder that led up outside the barn to the open doorway of the loft. He peered into the barn and saw that he would have a clear view into the stall where Lazzard and the girl were if he entered the loft.

He quickly told the two men what he planned to do, and after checking the idea, they both told him it could work. He nodded, and stepped away, making for the ladder. He ascended slowly, and when he reached the doorway of the loft he flattened himself and crawled in. He started inching over the straw covered floor, and boards creaked under his weight. He slowed his progress until he was hardly moving, and sweat began to run down his face. He holstered his gun and continued, his teeth clenched and high hopes in his heart.

It took him several long minutes to get clear of the doorway, and as he advanced into the loft he eased towards the open space over the centre of the stable floor. He pushed his Stetson off his head, and it hung by the chin strap. He could see into the first stall on the opposite side now, and he lifted his head slightly and peered along the line. He saw Letty standing as he had last seen her, but could not spot Lazzard.

Larew continued moving stealthily. He didn't care how long it took. He was going to assert his superiority over Ike Lazzard. His blood boiled when he thought of how he had knuckled under, but beneath his anger was the cold knowledge that had he stood up against the Lazy L they would have killed him. Perhaps that had been their intention. It would have suited Ben Lazzard if a killing had taken place over Letty. It would have solved the crooked rancher's problem of getting at him without it being obvious why.

He kept low as he inched forward, and as he eased himself up again he heard Lazzard yelling a warning. He guessed that some of the townsmen who were forming the posse had come to investigate the shooting. The sheriff would be there, and now they were crowding into the barn. Lazzard yelled for them to keep clear. Larew lifted himself and saw the youngster with his back to the wall of the stall, and the girl was cowering under the menace of the big gun in Lazzard's steady hand.

"Keep back, everyone," Ike Lazzard yelled. "I'll kill her if anyone tries anything."

"What is it you want?" a voice demanded, and John Larew recognised the sheriff's shaky tones.

"I wanta get outa here alive," Lazzard retorted. "Larew tried to kill me."

"Get rid of your gun and walk out," the sheriff retorted. "No one is gonna hurt you. Come on out."

"I'm staying here until Larew comes for me," the youngster replied, his tones changing. "I'm gonna kill that skunk."

"You better come out while you're able to," the sheriff warned.

"Go to hell," Lazzard shouted.

John Larew studied the stall. The girl was out of the line of fire, but Lazzard was pointing his gun at her. Could he shoot the weapon out of Lazzard's hand? A shot in the arm or the shoulder should do the trick. Larew sweated. If he missed then the girl he loved would surely take a slug.

He drew his gun and eased himself up on one knee. There were bales of straw piled haphazardly around the loft, and Larew was covered by one. He rested his gun-hand on the bale and drew a bead on Lazzard's right shoulder. He didn't want to kill the youngster, but he would if there was no other way. Ike Lazzard had been asking for something like this ever since he'd been old enough to raise hell.

Larew blinked his eyes, and restrained his breathing. He hoped Lazzard would not move in the last second. He gently squeezed his trigger, and the crash of the Colt shook the barn. A plume of gunsmoke belched from the muzzle of the gun, and Larew ducked to keep Lazzard in view. He saw the youngster jerk and swing halfway around from the girl under the heavy impact of the .45 slug, and the gun fell from Lazzard's hand.

Larew pushed himself upright, thumbing back his hammer.

"Get outa there, Letty," he yelled, and the girl fled blindly. He covered the youngster and waited. "What are you gonna do, Ike?" he demanded. "You wanta walk out there to the sheriff or die?"

"I'll surrender," Lazzard called. "Don't shoot. I'm hit bad. I'll give up."

"Walk out front then," Larew commanded, and he kept the youngster under the menace of his Colt as Lazard obeyed. The next moment some possemen had run forward and taken hold of him, and Larew sighed heavily and relaxed. He holstered his gun and made his way to the inner ladder and descended to the floor of the stable.

Letty Haig came running into his arms, and Larew held her close while he watched the sheriff take Lazzard away. The cowboys who had ridden into town with him came crowding around, demanding to be told what had happened, and Larew gave them an account.

"That's settled Ike Lazzard," John Larew commented crisply. "It should have been done long ago. Now we've got to get out to the Lazy L and deal with his father. If you're all ready then let's get moving. We can't afford to take any chances with that tough bunch."

The crowding men agreed, and turned away. They went out to the street and collected their mounts, and Larew wiped the sweat from his forehead. He glanced at the girl's pale face.

"Letty," he said gently. "Let's have no more talk about you marrying Lazzard. We both know the rights of it, and when this has been settled I'll come back again and ask you to marry me. You cut along back to the store now and keep your fingers crossed for us. With a little luck we'll be able to finish this off without too much trouble."

But he didn't believe that as he went for his own

mount. He watched the girl going along the sidewalk, and shook his head as he turned and headed for the law office where the posse was mounted and growing impatient. It was going to be a tough fight.

CHAPTER 9

WHEN Buck's senses returned to him he became aware of the pain in his chest and head. He opened his eyes slowly, grunting at the agony boiling up inside him. So he was still alive! That was his first thought. Then he wondered why. He put a hand to his forehead, and felt a patch of dried blood. He groaned again as he tried to struggle into a sitting position. Then he saw Ben Lazzard lounging in the shade of a rock. Drago Heppell was stretched out on his back beside the rancher. Heppell wasn't dead. He was smoking a cigarette. His shirt had been ripped into strips, and was now tied around his chest and left shoulder. There were bloodstains upon the thin material.

As Buck moved Ben Lazzard lifted a Colt and menaced him with it. Buck looked around and saw Roan Morrell lying out in the sun. He grunted as pain clawed at his chest wound with ragged edges as he tried to get to his feet. He made it, but felt weak and unsteady. He inspected the bloodstain on his left ribs and found a bullet graze. It was a deep, nasty wound, but the bleeding had stopped. He lumbered forward towards Roan Morrell.

"Don't bother," Ben Lazzard called. "He's dead as mutton."

Buck turned towards the rock and stumbled forward. Heppell was regarding him with pure hatred showing on his pale face and glittering in his dark eyes.

"Kill him, Ben, and have done with it," the gunman snarled. "You know how dangerous he is."

"You don't have to tell me," Lazzard said. "I knew

that the minute I laid eyes on him. But we got to find out how much they know back in town. Morrell was following us, and Larew shows up behind him, and wearing a law badge. They suspect us, Drago, and we've got to find out how much they know."

"Stop playing around then and get on with it," Heppell said testily. "I want to be getting back to the ranch. I reckon it's time to pull out. I'll want my cut of the dough and fast."

"You can leave whenever you like," Lazzard said, smiling. "You know where the dough is cached. Go help yourself to your share and beat it."

"I'll do that," Heppell said, "when I feel like climbing into my saddle."

Larew sank to the ground in the shade of a smaller rock about six feet from Ben Lazzard. The rancher twisted to keep his gun on Buck, and there was a tight grin on Lazzard's thin lips.

"Okay," he rapped, "start talking. What were you and Morrell doing behind us?"

"Just taking the air," Buck replied. "Have you got a guilty conscience, Lazzard?"

"What are you wearing that law star for?" Lazzard went on.

"Decided to pitch in and help the local law. They could sure do with it."

"So what are you riding around the country for, taking the air? What do you think, Larew, that I crawled out of some hole in the ground? You can't fool me. That part about taking the star to help is true enough, I reckon, but you ain't riding around for your health."

"If he is then he made a bad mistake," Heppell grated. "It's turned plumb unlucky for him."

"You and Morrell were following us," Lazzard said. "What for?"

"I don't see why I shouldn't lay my cards on the table," Buck said, smiling thinly. He leaned back against the rock and closed his eyes for a moment. His head was aching intolerably, and the glare of the sun overhead was hurting his eyes. "You're guilty of robbing the bank and killing Anders, the banker. We know that, and all I had to do was trail you and catch you picking up the dough where you cached it last night."

Heppell started cursing fitfully, and thrust himself to his feet. He stared down at Lazzard, his pale face twisted with fury.

"Damn you, Ben," he rapped. "I allus did tell you that one day you would get too careless, and now it's happened. I'm getting out of this neck of the woods before a posse shows up."

"Hold your hosses a minute, Drago," Lazzard snapped. He kept his eyes on Buck's sweating face. "How did the sheriff get suspicious?"

"It's a long story," Buck retorted, "but I'll give you the bones of it." He went on to tell them tersely how he had sneaked into the Lazy L with Morrell, and learned about the bid to poison the waterhole. When he told of riding to warn Clanton, and of the arrangements he made with the Circle C rancher, Ben Lazzard started cursing. Buck grinned and continued, and brought them up to date with the happenings, explaining how he and Morrell had seen them the night before, riding hell for leather through the night; how he and Morrell had checked their hotel room to make sure it was Ben Lazzard who had been on the trail. When he fell silent Heppel began to rant.

"I told you we should have dropped that dough into your cabin and made it straight back to the hotel," the gunman snarled. "Damn your hide, Ben, for trying to play it too smart."

"I still maintain I was right," Lazzard snapped. "If we hung around town with all that dough someone might have seen us making for the cabin. We might have been spotted sneaking inside with all the bags. That would have finished us. It was just bad luck Larew and Morrell had to be on the trail when we passed by."

"That damn crew you've got out at the ranch," Heppell said. "They should have been guarding the place. Now we better cut our losses and get clear of the county. You know what's gonna happen when Clanton and Sutton get together. They're gonna ride on to the Lazy L and tear it to pieces. You've shore been giving both spreads some hell lately, and they'll be around to pay you back."

"I don't think so," Lazzard said. He grinned harshly as he told them how he had paid Pete Roscoe to be on hand when Clanton's crew rode into Sutton's place. "You see, it don't make much difference what happens between Clanton and Sutton. When Roscoe cuts loose there's gonna be a war."

"What about the sheriff?" Heppell demanded. "He knows Morrell and Larew followed us out of town. He ain't gonna be long behind them with a posse."

Buck didn't think Wickup would ride out with a posse. The lawman was going to stick around town until Buck returned with news. But he didn't say that.

"That was the idea," he told them, smiling thinly. "I was to come on ahead and try to catch you lifting that loot, and the sheriff will be coming on with a posse, in case you decide against touching the dough until the heat was off. If that happened we were gonna arrest you."

"I'm gonna put an end to you right now," Heppell snapped, pulling his gun, and Buck tensed, his face suddenly serious.

"Hold it, you fool," Lazzard snapped, springing to his feet. "Ain't you got no sense, Drago? If this situation is as Larew says then we're gonna need a hole card in our hand. We'll keep Larew prisoner, just in case things get a bit tight."

"I reckon you're wasting time," the gunman rasped. "The only thing we can do now is collect that dough and haul our freight. If Clanton and Sutton ain't dead then they're gonna be after your hide as well as the law. You reckon you're smart, Ben. Well show it now. Get to hell outa here."

Lazzard shook his head obstinately. Buck nodded to himself. He had summed up this man properly in the first place. Lazzard wasn't going to turn his back on anything. He would have to be killed to be stopped. But he was in a tight spot himself, and unless he outsmarted Lazzard then he was slated for a bullet. He didn't want to get taken to the Lazy L, where the rest of Lazzard's tough crew were waiting. That would make the odds far too great. He cursed his aching head. The chest wound was very painful, but it wasn't bothering him any right now. He'd taken worse in the Rangers. But his head was throbbing madly, and he couldn't think as fast as normally.

"I can see what's in your mind by what's on your face," Ben Lazzard said. "You're thinking that you're gonna turn the tables on me. But I'm too smart for you, hombre. I'm gonna take you back to my place and see how you get on with my crew. Get over there to your hoss and climb into the saddle. Don't try anything or I'll bust your spine for you."

"You're crazy, Ben," Drago Heppell rasped angrily. "What the hell! You must be going soft in your old age. We're wasting time right now, and there could be a posse on our tail from town and two outfits chasing in from the other direction. I'm gonna make a run for it. Let's get to the dough and split it up. You can do what you damn well like, but I'm quitting, and fast."

They mounted, and Buck took up his reins.

"Go on ahead, and not too fast," Lazzard ordered. "You just look like you're fixing to run for it and I'll start shooting. I ain't seen a hoss yet that could outrun a bullet, so remember that."

"I'm several kinds of a fool and always have been," Buck retorted, "but I'm not that stupid. Okay, so you're holding a winning hand right now. I can play according to the cards I hold."

Heppell cursed and kneed his horse ahead of Buck, and started fast along the ravine. Lazzard motioned for Buck to follow, and moved in behind when Buck complied. Buck noticed that the rancher held his Colt, and the steady muzzle was gaping at him.

They went on for ten minutes, and came to a place where the high wall of the ravine was broken away on the right hand. A narrow path snaked up over the low bank, and Buck reined up when he saw Drago Heppell leave his saddle and reel across to a pile of rocks. Lazzard reined up, and kept well out of distance. Buck narrowed his eyes when he saw that Lazzard had no intention of giving him any kind of a chance. This was going to be much more tougher than he had figured. His chances were slim, and he could see it.

Heppell disappeared among the rocks, and was gone several long moments. Then the gunman re-appeared, and he was carrying half a dozen money bags that had been roped together. He dumped them on the hard ground beside his horse, and grinned up at Lazzard.

"Better keep an eye on him, Ben, while I divvy up this dough. We know each other well enough to know that one wouldn't double-cross the other. I'll take a rough half, and then I'm pulling out. I reckon your share is gonna be wasted though. It'll wind up back in the bank when the law gets you."

"I'm not quitting," Lazzard snapped. "I ain't finished around here, not by a long rope. Anyways, Ike is still in town. You think I'd run without him along?"

Buck sat his mount and watched the feverish movements of Drago Heppell. The gunman opened up all six bags and shook out their contents. Buck thinned his lips, his eyes narrowed and bright. There was a haul and a half down there on the ground. Lazzard began chuckling harshly. Heppell looked up, his face showing eagerness and impatience. He began sorting through the money, ignoring the pile of coins and concentrating upon the neat wads of notes. He quickly split them into two piles.

"Yours and mine, Ben," he said at length. "Pity you won't be able to spend yours. You're playing a fool game now, and you know it."

"No one's gonna run me out, Drago," Lazzard replied with a grin. "Put mine back in the bags and pass them over. I'm not taking any chances with Larew. He's riding with me to my place."

"You are a fool, and no mistake," Heppell said. "What do you think will happen if anyone shows up at the Lazy L and catch you with him on your hands?"

"It'll mean a fight, and that's something I ain't never ducked in my life," Lazzard said. "Now you better get your dough together and start moving out."

Heppell returned the money to the various bags, and tied Lazzard's share together. He lifted the weighty haul and brought it to Lazzard's mount. Ben Lazzard fixed it with a loose piece of rope to his saddlehorn.

"So long, Drago," he said. "It's been nice knowing you. Watch your trail."

"You're the one who's gonna have to do that," the gunman replied, "and it hurts me to think of all that dough you got there going back to the ones we stole it from."

"They'll have to kill me to get it," Lazzard retorted, "and I ain't dead yet."

Heppell fixed his money to his saddlehorn and stepped up into his saddle. He stared at Buck for a moment, no expression in his dark, cold eyes. Then he grinned at Lazzard.

"So long, Ben," he grunted. "Might see you around."

Lazzard nodded, his eyes fixed upon Buck.

"Get moving, Larew," the rancher commanded. "You know where the Lazy L is. Head for it, and if you wanta live then don't give me any cause to kill you."

Buck shook his reins and his mount started forward. He cast a backward glance at Heppell, and saw the gunman riding west. He continued along the ravine with Lazzard close behind. There were furious thoughts going around in Buck's head. Now Heppell was gone there was only Lazzard to worry about. He knew that he couldn't afford to take any chances with the rancher, but the odds were halved, and now he could watch out for his chance to turn the tables on Lazzard.

"Shake it up a bit," Lazzard called suddenly. "I want to get home. If you've stirred up things like you say you have then there'll be gunsmoke drifting across the Lazy L, and I wanta be there to handle my outfit. They're a tough bunch, but they ain't got much in the way of brains."

Buck obeyed. He had already decided that he wouldn't get any kind of a chance to beat Lazzard out here. Although riding into the Lazy L would bring the rest of the outfit against him he knew he would have more chance to escape while in their midst than here. With some of his crew around, Lazzard might get careless, and Buck only needed half a chance.

The ground sloped upwards, and the walls of the ravine lowered. They eventually emerged from the deep cover, and Buck reined up.

"Keep moving," Lazzard snarled. "Don't try any tricks."

"Which way?" Buck demanded. "I'm a stranger to this range."

"You sure enough knew your way around my place," the rancher replied, grinning tightly. "You've caused a helluva lot of trouble for me." He thinned his lips, staring around with his blue eyes narrowed and glittering. "Ride in that direction, towards that hill in the distance. We'll pass to the right of that, then head south-west."

Buck took up his reins and prepared to move on. His teeth were gritted against the pain in him. He heard an angry crackle in his right ear, and frowned as he twisted in his saddle. He'd had enough lead thrown at him in his time to know the sound of it. He spotted gunsmoke rising from a screen of bushes a hundred yards off, and in the same instant he heard Ben Lazzard cry out. He swung back to face the rancher, and saw Lazzard going out of his saddle, and there was blood on the rancher's shirt front.

Without hesitation Buck kicked his feet free of his stirrups and dived for cover. He hit the ground hard and hurt himself upon landing, but he kept moving, and rolled away from his horse as a rifle slug came snarling in search of his flesh. He scurried back into the mouth of the ravine, and looked for Ben Lazzard. His eyes narrowed when he saw the rancher sprawled out on the ground in the open. Lazzard seemed to be unconscious.

Buck stared at the rising puff of smoke that marked the position of the ambusher, and his mind worked overtime in an attempt to read the significance of the attack. Was it one of Clanton's men, or a rider from Sutton's Broken S? He moistened his dry lips. He needed a gun, and the nearest was in Lazzard's holster. The rancher's horse had halted some yards away, and Buck could see the butt of a Winchester protruding from the saddleboot. He clenched his teeth. It was too dangerous to make an attempt to grab it. There was too much open ground, and the rifleman had proved himself a good shot. But he tensed himself. He could get out of this predicament once he got his hands on a gun. He would have to take a chance and make a run for Lazzard's Colt. The rancher was half a dozen yards out from the mouth of the ravine, but with a hidden rifleman waiting for any move it seemed like six miles.

He took a deep breath and steeled himself for the effort, and Ben Lazzard spoke to him.

"Don't do it, Larew," the rancher called hoarsely. "I'm not out of it. I'm trying to draw him into the open. Just keep still. I've got my eye on you, too. Try anything and I'll plug you."

Buck relaxed. He grinned tightly. Lazzard was proving himself to be tough and obdurate. The rancher was bleeding badly from his wound, but he had been the only one unwounded in the shooting in the ravine. Buck stiffened as he thought about that. Supposing their ambusher was Drago Heppell? The gunman had showed reluctance to leave Lazzard's share of the money. He had figured it was on its way back to the bank in Rainbow Creek.

"Got any idea who it is?" he called to the waiting rancher.

"Don't make any difference," Lazzard replied implacably. "I'll kill him soon as he shows himself. Now you stay quiet and let him get enough confidence to come out."

Buck wondered about that. If it was Heppell out there then he would know that only Lazzard was armed. Anyone else would figure that he had an armed man pinned in the ravine. He studied the position from where the shots had been fired, and figured that the ambusher could have enough cover to enable him to sneak away from that spot unseen. He was about to call to Lazzard, telling him about it, when a bullet struck the ground at his side, piercing his empty holster. He jerked in surprise, twisting as he hurled himself flat, and he rolled on to his back and saw Drago Heppell standing on the rim above him. The gunman was grinning viciously, his smoking Colt steady in his expert right hand.

Buck lay still, hoping that Heppell would figure that he was finished. Lazzard should be buying into it any time, and he wanted to be flat while these two old friends traded hot lead. He had his eyes closed, but he could see Heppell's ominous figure through his slitted lids.

Heppell was coming down the bank, leaning far back to keep his balance on the decline. Buck waited for Lazzard to start shooting. But the rancher wasn't ready to take a hand yet. Heppell paused at the bottom of the bank and stared at Buck, and for a moment Buck thought the gunman was going to put another slug into him. He tensed his muscles for the strike of the lead, but Heppell raised his eyes and stared at Lazzard lying out in the open. A grin came to his harsh face as he looked at the rancher's horse, standing hipshot in the sunlight, with half a fortune in the bags suspended from the saddlehorn.

The gunman started forward, and the toe of his boot kicked against Buck's left elbow. With a desperate surge of strength, Buck seized hold of Heppell's ankle and heaved the gunman off balance. Heppell twisted like a cat as he came down, and the deadly muzzle of his Colt swung quickly to cover Buck. There was the booming crash of a shot and Heppell's gun flew from his hand. Heppell's eyes widened with shock, and his face showed overwhelming surprise.

"You dirty, double-crossing skunk!" Ben Lazzard roared, and Buck eased back, gasping for breath, glancing around at the rancher, who was getting unsteadily to his feet. "Drago Heppell! After all I've done for you. This is the way you repay my friendship. Get away from him, Larew. I'm gonna shoot out his goddamned eyes."

"You're a damn fool," Heppell said. "You would have been killed anyway, and lost the dough. I figured I could put it to good use."

"You know any prayers then you better start saying them," Lazzard snarled. "Get out of it, Larew, or you'll stop a slug."

Buck slithered back, pushing himself to his feet. He kept backing off, and halted when he felt the heel of his right boot touching the hardness of Heppell's discarded gun. He watched both men with deep concentration. If he was fast enough he could come out on top. But he had to play it careful. Lazzard wouldn't hesitate to kill him.

The rancher was incensed by Heppell's attempt to double-cross him, and it seemed that he wasn't going to kill the gunman without first berating him for his underhand game. Buck listened, tensed and ready, but Lazzard was no fool, and half his attention was on Buck himself. Buck dropped slowly to his knees, hanging his head, but he watched Lazzard intently.

"Did he hit you, Larew?" the rancher demanded.

"Yeah," Buck replied huskily. "But I figure you're gonna kill me anyway, so what's the odds?"

"You're a man after my own heart," Lazzard said, grinning. He lifted his left hand and pressed the palm against his chest, covering the spot where Heppell's bullet had hit him. He reeled slightly, and Buck let his right hand flop down to the ground. The knuckles of his hand touched the hot steel of the fallen gun. He gritted his teeth as he watched the grim scene before him.

"You're a lowdown yaller skunk, Drago," Lazzard said. "Of all the men I ever knew you were the only one I figured I could trust. Now you pull a stunt like this, and for a couple of bags of lousy money. I'm gonna blast you for this. Anything else I could have overlooked, but this is lowdown."

"Get it over with then," Heppell snarled. "You don't have to give me a sermon, Ben. I made my play and lost out. Okay, so get it done."

"You start saying your prayers," the rancher commanded. "Where do you want it, Drago?"

"Don't let me suffer," the gunman retorted.

Buck listened to them, his amazement at their cold-blooded conversation almost overwhelming. He started his right hand outwards, the fingers crawling over the gun. He touched the butt and began to lift it, his eyes upon Ben Lazzard.

Lazzard's face began to tighten its expression. Buck could see the intention to shoot showing plainly in the haggard features. He started to lift the gun. He would have to wait until Lazzard fired before making his own move. Lazzard was fast and dangerous.

The rancher began to tighten his trigger finger. His teeth showed whitely as he grinned. Heppell tensed himself for the tearing impact of the heavy bullet, and Buck took a deep breath and prepared for his effort. Heppell suddenly dropped to his knees, holding out his arms to the determined rancher.

"Don't do it, Ben," he cried. "Let me go."

"Don't make me sick, Drago," the rancher snapped.

His face twisted with viciousness, and he fired. The crash of the shot blared out, and in the same instant, as Drago Heppell stiffened and jerked under the thudding bullet, Buck swept up his gunhand. He was tempted in that split second to put a slug through Lazzard's chest, but he shifted his aim and went for the gunhand. The gun hammered powerfully, and he clicked his teeth together as Lazzard went rolling over, his reflexes faster than a cat's.

The rancher came up on one knee, his teeth bared, the gun in his hand coming up to level at Buck. A tension was swelling inside Buck. He threw himself flat, cocking the gun as he did so, and Lazzard fired. There was a flashing pain across Buck's right shoulder, and he almost dropped the gun in shock, but he set his teeth and let drive at the rancher. He aimed for the right shoulder, and Ben Lazzard let out a howl of pain and rage and twisted away, his gun dropping to the ground. But Lazzard was not done. He made a grab at the fallen weapon.

Buck fired again, his slug striking the gun and causing it to skitter several feet away from Lazzard's clawing fingers.

"Don't try it again," he warned, his tones rasping through the dying echoes. "I don't want to kill you, Lazzard. I want to see you stand trial for what you've done around here. Get up and do it slow. Get your hands up and stand still. I guess this just about takes care of you."

"Don't be a fool," the rancher said harshly. "You can't hope to beat my outfit. They'll ride into town and destroy it the minute they hear that I'm in jail. And by the looks of it they're on their way over here right now. Look, Larew, riders coming, and they're my men."

Buck heard the sound of approaching hoofs, and it

sounded like a big bunch coming. He thinned his lips. Just his luck! He took a quick look in the direction the sounds were coming from, and spotted nearly a score of riders. The next instant Ben Lazzard was crashing into him, desperate to get the upper hand. Buck gave way instead of fighting, and went down on his back with Lazzard sprawling atop him. The impact of the fall, coupled with the weight of Lazzard's heavy body, drove the breath out of his lungs. The muzzle of the gun jammed against Lazzard's chest, and Buck tried to twist, to get it away before the gun exploded. But Lazzard was intent upon beating him, and kept crowding. Buck could feel growing pressure on his trigger finger, and he tried desperately to get the gun away. Then it bucked in his hand. The crash of the shot was muffled between their straining bodies, and Ben Lazzard let out a screech of agony. He stiffened, then relaxed, and rolled off Buck.

The sound of the approaching riders was getting louder. They had been attracted by the shooting. Buck pushed himself wearily to one knee. It looked like his luck had deserted him, but he would take as many of Lazzard's crew with him as he could. They would kill him. There was no doubt about that, but they'd know they'd been in a fight by the time he got through with them. He cocked the Colt, glancing aside at the fallen rancher. A second look wasn't needed to tell him that Lazzard was dead.

Buck looked ahead, narrowing his eyes. Sweat was pouring down his face, and his body seemed to be filled with pain. He squinted at the oncoming men, and caught the glint of sunlight upon naked steel. He bared his teeth. Some of these men would soon be joining Lazzard and his double-crossing partner Heppell in hell. There was plenty of room there for this kind.

The riders drew nearer, and Buck thought he recognised some of the leading faces. The next instant he was pushing himself upright, holstering his gun and lifting a hand to wave. There was the sheriff and his brother John in the lead. This was a posse!

Buck relaxed then. He sighed long and hard, and the rest of his strength seemed to fade with the breath. He staggered to a rock and sat down heavily. He stared at the two dead robbers, and glanced at the horse holding Lazzard's share of the loot. He had come into this county to help his brother ranch on the Bar Sixty, and instead he had found a pile of trouble waiting to be shot to pieces. Well the posse should be able to handle the Lazzard crew at the Lazy L. Without their boss the gunmen would not have any heart to fight for a dead cause. That seemed to be the end of it, he thought tiredly. It suddenly came to him that he hadn't alighted for more than a couple of minutes since he'd been in the county. But now the sounds of the shooting had faded completely, and there was peace once more on the range. He hoped it would stay like that. He'd come through more than his share of gunsmoke. As the posse came up and halted his trembling fingers unpinned the deputy star he was wearing. Bub Wickup and the rest of the townsmen could handle it from here on in. . . .